ON YOUR MARKS

ON YOUR MARKS

THE BOOK OF CRAZY EXAM STORIES

INTRODUCTION BY
ROOPA PAI

talking
CUB

TALKING CUB
Published by Speaking Tiger Publishing Pvt. Ltd
4381/4, Ansari Road, Daryaganj
New Delhi 110002

First published in Talking Cub by Speaking Tiger in 2018

ISBN: 978-93-87693-31-9
eISBN: 978-93-87693-30-2

10 9 8 7 6 5 4 3 2 1

Typeset in Lora Regular by SÜRYA, New Delhi
Printed at Sanat Printers, Kundli

This is a work of fiction. Names, characters, places and
incidents either are the product of the author's imagination
or are used fictitiously, and any resemblance
to actual persons, living or dead, events or
locales is entirely coincidental.

Contents

Introduction

I'm genuinely sorry to kick things off this way, but it's likely that what I'm about to say is going to make me very unpopular with young readers. So I'll just say it in a rush and hope you won't get it— Ithinkexamsareaverygoodideaindeed.

There. I said it.

I say this despite hating, absolutely *hating*, exams myself. For years and years after I'd written (what so far has been) the last academic exam of my life, I suffered what is today acronymically called PTSD or Post-Traumatic Stress Disorder. (On a side note, why does everyone love acronyms so much these days? How can an average—or even reasonably intelligent—person keep track of them? The moment you think you've got your acronyms figured, they introduce a whole new set, and you've to start from scratch again! Ugh!) Even up until my late thirties, I would wake up in the middle of the night, bathed in a cold sweat, my mouth dry, my heart racing, my palms clammy, screaming, because, in my nightmare, I had just discovered—*on the morning of the final exam!*—that I had got my timetable mixed up and therefore studied for the wrong paper! (Okay, maybe I am lying about the screaming part, but the rest of it is absolutely, one hundred per cent true).

I say this (that exams are a good idea) despite the fact that, quite apart from the bone-chilling, soul-killing stuff they wreak on you in the years *after* you're done with them, exams are monstrous things even while they are going on. More than the stress of actually studying for them (I'm never *ever* going to finish studying all of it/OMG! I forgot about the diagrams and the map work!/How in heck is it going to help me in later life to know at what precise moment a train rushing from Place A to Place B is going to collide with another train coming at it from Place B to Place A, when 'Engine driver' is not one of my preferred career choices?) is the guilt (about that TV show you could have done without watching, that extra hour you stayed in bed, the parent whose wise advice you did not heed, and all those days and days you skived off applying yourself to your books because you were doing something far, far more interesting) and the disproportionate, irrational fear (I'm going to fail! I'm going to fail! I'm going to fail!) that accompanies every single exam.

(Yes, I *am quite aware that my sentences are way too long, punctuated way too often by annoying parentheses and dashes, and way too full of random off-topic soliloquies, but since I'm the one writing the introduction, and I like to write like this, I'm afraid you are just going to have to deal with it. It's good practice for dealing with other unsavoury things in life. Exams, for example.)*

I say this (that exams are a good idea) despite the fact that exam papers are often set by cranky adults who get a perverse joy out of rooting around in the darkest corners of the textbook to find the smallest, most-insignificant-looking grey boxes whose content you have been told very specifically (by your seniors) you will *never* be quizzed on, and ask you a question from there; or set you a problem from the *exact* Maths exercise that your classmates (from the other section) have told you is not part of the portions (according to their Maths teacher). Needless to say, that same paper-setting adult will be in a particularly grouchy mood when she is correcting your paper (why does it always happen when it's *your* paper? We shall never know—put it down to one of life's great mysteries), and will cut marks—a half mark here, two marks there—for no reason that anyone (and especially you) can fathom, while giving that classmate you hate full marks *for the exact same answer.*

And I say this (that exams are a good idea) even though exams cause parents to be on their absolutely worst behaviour with you—like asking you 252 times if you have sharpened your pencils/packed your compass/carried enough pens/flushed after you went poo-poo (I know, no connection at all—it's just that *their* brains get so addled when *you're* having exams that they don't often know what they are saying, so forgive the poor lambs), or saying to you, when you're absolutely losing it five minutes before you leave for school on an exam day, something you know perfectly well already, like—'Well, if you hadn't spent the whole of last evening texting someone on your phone...but it's too late to do anything about that now.'

So yes, as I have established rather elaborately, I do say it (that exams are a good idea), despite everything.

Why do I think exams are a good idea? Many reasons, but the main one is the most pragmatic one: exams are not going away any time soon, so if you don't quickly start believing that they are good for you and find reasons to back up that argument, you might end up becoming hopelessly depressed. And no one wants that.

Secondly, one needs to have some way to check if a student has actually learnt what she is supposed to have at every stage of the learning journey, and exams are a good way to do that. You see, formal education, which is the kind of education you get in school (as opposed to informal education, which is the kind of education you get from your friends, nature, playing sports, talking to random people, or just hanging out in the world for long enough), is based entirely on building knowledge layer by layer. In other words, if your first layer of learning isn't strong enough, if you haven't, for instance, learnt to read, write or do basic arithmetic by the time you have finished second grade, it is pointless trying to build the next layer—reading and understanding bigger words and ideas, doing more complex arithmetic like multiplication and division, etc. If you insist on doing so, sooner or later, the tottery building that is your formal education will fall down in a heap.

(Now, we can argue all day about whether formal education itself is a good thing. But if your parents are anything like mine were—i.e., they have enrolled you in school and plan to keep you there for several years—this is an argument to no purpose. Your parents are unlikely to pull you out of school however brilliantly you make your case, because the real reason they love the idea of formal education is a selfish, selfish one—it is the only legal and socially acceptable way they know to keep you out of their hair for eight hours a day.)

The other reason I think that exams are a good idea is this: they teach you, apart from Maths and Science and Social Studies, a ton of extra-curricular skills that are most useful in life. **Hard work**, for instance. Or the fine art of **time management**—how to portion out the, well, portions, so that you can give them all a good once-over before the exams begin; how to allot time to different sections of the question paper so that you finish answering it well in time, while still leaving enough time for 'revision', and so on. Also, **prioritizing**, which is the science of quick and strategic decision-making—now that you have under three hours of prep left, say, which lessons should you go over again—the ones which are likely to earn you the most marks, or the ones you know least well? And most importantly,

discipline—for it is a sad fact that it is most often the student who listens carefully in class, does his or her lessons regularly, and turns in work on time who does better at exams than the last-minute crammer.

Of course, simply telling yourself that you are learning all these wonderful skills is not going to make exams any less bearable while you're actually taking them. But maybe you can take some small comfort in the fact that they don't just exist in the Muggle world—everyone at Hogwarts had to take exams too!

Here's another thought that may make taking exams less painful—tell yourself, over and over, that you are not competing with anyone but yourself. That you are not studying because you want to come first or get full marks or do better than someone else. That you are studying simply because it is your responsibility as a student to do so. Think you can do that? If you can, you are already a winner.

Because really, *really-really*, it doesn't matter a whit how many marks someone else gets, and it doesn't matter a wiggle whether you top the class or not. In the end, what matters is that you can tell yourself, hand on heart, that you have put in your very best effort to learn your lessons well, that you haven't cheated on yourself (by playing a game on your phone during study time, when no one was looking, say) and that you have prepared for your exams in the very best way you know how.

Plus, there is nothing to beat that rare and absolute high you feel when you look down at a question paper in an exam that you have prepared well for, and realize that you know the answer to every single question! It makes all the hard work, all the sleepless nights, all the hours of beavering away at a tough Maths problem until you cracked it, all the trouble you took to cook up creative acronyms (sigh! Here they come again!) to help you remember which states have black cotton soil and which are the noble gases in the periodic table, completely worthwhile. You may not end up getting full marks on that paper eventually, but that surge of heady adrenalin you felt when you looked down at that paper, that warm rush of self-confidence, that sense of happy achievement—'I *got* this, man!'—no one can take that away from you, ever. That's something to aim for, right?

And last, but definitely not the least, exams are such a universal phenomenon and such a big—and traumatic—part of most adults' memories that they spawn exciting and fun anthologies like the one you are holding in your hands right now! So grab a tall glass of something cold and refreshing, sit down in your favourite corner, and proceed to enjoy a right royal treat of 'exam' stories that span the gamut from laugh-out-loud funny, ghostly, geeky and extra-terrestrial-ly to touching, fantastical, hair-raising, and more, laid out especially for you by a bunch of the country's most talented authors for children.

For let's face it, we live in testing times, and one of the few things that can help us through them is a ripping good yarn.

Roopa Pai

What Happens to Children Who Say They Are Going to Fail Their Exams but Then Stand First

JERRY PINTO

The exams are coming,
My head is humming,
With things I just didn't mug,
But the girl who stands first,
Says in a tearful burst,
'Oh man, I'm sure to plug.'

The tests draw near,
Once more I fear,
The red marks on my report,
But the girl who stands first
(For her blood I thirst)
Declares she'll score a zot.

When the reports are posted,
And my backside's toasted,
Once more she will declare,
'It's just sheer luck
That I didn't duck'
Though her marks are right up there.

This lugubrious twit,
Would worry a bit,
If she heard the tale of Zenobia,
A girl who claimed,
Her brain has been maimed,
by examination phobia.

Zinny, need I say
Never could play
Since she was so busy mugging
But when a test neared
Zinny was afeared
That she was going to be plugging.

Each final exam
The same old scam
Dear Zinny was sure to moot.
Until one year,
Nemesis, I fear,
Decided to give her the boot.

The teacher was old
I make so bold
To say she hadn't a clue.
With a tired air,
She climbed to her chair
And stuck there, as if with glue.

The paper fell
A cold death knell
Upon each waiting table.
All heads down
Fear all around
This is the stuff of fable.

Q1 is a zonker
Q2 is a conker
Q3's a hard nut to crack.
As for Q4
I simply don't know.
This paper will break your back.

Then through the hall
A mighty bawl
A scream of dread surprise
It's Zinny shrieking
Like a demon squeaking
At a djinn extracting its eyes.

Zinny's here, Zinny's there
Zinny's under her chair
She's screaming as loud as a banshee
There's froth at her mouth
Her mind's going south
For Zinny can never fail, can she?

The teacher's calls
Echo down the halls
As she gets help for Zenobia
The docs look grave,
'No chance to save
The cortico-spasmoidal lobe, here.'

Ten minutes after
We're all going dafter
Trying to sort out the mess
A teacher announces
With regretful flounces,
'Kids, here's a stop press.

'Class Six may stop
Having a pop
At the paper we have distributed.
We printed the plate
Meant for class Eight.
The typist has been executed.'

What happened to Zin?
In the loony bin
I'm sorry to say they locked her
She sits there now
A quiet old cow
Supervised by a nice old doctor.

For many a day
She stayed that way
Serene as an egg newly laid.
She's quite calm
The only alarm,
Should doc say, 'Tests to be made.'

Then old Zenobia
Shows off her phobia
Of the test, the quiz, the exam
Even a stool sample
Gives her ample
Opportunity for the jimjams.

So if you've the kind
Of vomitous mind
Who says she is sure to fail
And quietly goes
And scores in crores
Remember Zenobia's tale.

A Brief History of Exams

ANSHUMANI RUDDRA

The tyranny of exams is not new. Grown-ups have been burdening children with tests, assessments and examinations since time immemorial. In this essay, I will try and highlight the key events throughout human history that have led to my current predicament:

- writing a 1,000-word essay (aaarrrggghhh!)
- on a unique topic of my own choosing (really— you couldn't have given me something easy and straightforward—like my favourite superhero movie, or a cricket match?)
- for an examination I don't care much about (I don't!)
  —A *disgruntled grade 8 student*

60,000 Years Ago
Somewhere in East Africa
Fire had been accidentally discovered. But it was important to be able to reproduce this accident.

Common methods of creating a fire included striking two sharp stones together and creating a spark that could be used to burn dried twigs and grass.

Young children were expected to know this. And so, the first test was created. Grown-ups would stand around children and encourage them to set things on fire. This started out as a fun activity and led to community building and family bonding (on a side note, why don't parents encourage their kids to start fires in this day and age? We are missing out on a truly spectacular learning experience.)

But leave it to adults to suck the fun out of anything interesting. Someone came up with the harebrained idea to see who could create a fire faster. Competition was introduced, and anxious parents would wring their hands as their kids tried to prove that they were better pyromaniacs than other children. Speed testing was all the rage at the dawn of civilization.

Huddled in caves, mothers could often be heard whispering to fathers: 'Sharmaji's son can light a fire faster than our Bittu! What will we do? Should we find a new fire coach for him?'

30,000 Years Ago
Somewhere in South-western Europe
This is the first recorded instance of children having nightmares about exams. What is crazy is that similar nightmares were being reported at the same time across different human tribes across the world. Here are a few samples:

- I could see all the children standing in the big cave at the end of the forest. They had fresh paint and brushes made from bison tails. They were painting mammoths and bears. Samuel sir, our drawing teacher, was walking around and grading the drawings. I did not have my paint and brushes. I didn't even know that the drawing test was today. I was going to fail! I started screaming. And that's when I woke up, drenched in sweat.
- I was late for my berry-picking test. I had woken up late and now had to run to the other end of the forest where the wild berries grew. All the boys and girls from my class were picking berries and sorting them when I reached the clearing. They all turned simultaneously, pointed at me and started laughing. I looked down and realized I was stark naked! In my hurry I had forgotten to put my clothes on. I woke up.

From turning up late (and naked), to forgetting that there was a test in the first place or running out of time while all your friends breezed through their tests was a common theme across all these nightmares. 30,000 years later nothing has changed. Even though she doesn't have to give exams any more (because she is a grown-up), my mom still has these nightmares.

10,000 Years Ago
Somewhere in China
The last ice age was a golden period for assessments and tests. Because of the freezing conditions and

limited things to do in the open, adults were finally able to put their heads together and come up with innovative ways of making life truly difficult for children everywhere.

This period produced the following kinds of examinations:

- Oral—children were expected to memorize names of animals, birds, trees, food items, location of various water sources and gods (grown-ups were becoming big on religion during this period)
- Practical—making clay pots, jewellery and figurines out of bones were the most common form of punishment (err... I mean examinations)
- Multiple Choice Questions—a few examples will illustrate the plight of children during the last ice age:

  o If a woolly mammoth is chasing you, what is your best course of action:

  a) Run away
  b) Hold your ground
  c) Find a sabre-toothed tiger to scare away the mammoth
  d) Turn around and pat the mammoth*

  o If the woolly mammoth has caught you and wrapped its trunk around you, what is your best course of action:

a) Stop wriggling, it might drop you
b) Wriggle a lot, it might get irritated and drop you
c) Find a sharp object and poke the mammoth's trunk#
d) None of the above—you are already dead

- Word Problems—these would go on to truly become the bane of existence for children everywhere. A choice example:

  o Li was twice his sister's age in the year Xi lost his big left toe to frostbite. If Li's sister was four seasons old back then, in which harvest season do you think will he be chased by an angry woolly mammoth?@

4,500 Years Ago
Egypt

Writing on clay tablets and large leaves (papyrus) was by now very common. Grown-ups had started keeping track of time through sundials and hourglasses. Timed written tests became the norm during this period.

Knowledge by now had been categorized into various subjects:

- Languages (writing and reading about crocodiles in the river Nile)
- Science (the study of crocodiles in the river Nile)
- Mathematics (counting the number of crocodiles in the river Nile)

- Astronomy (looking at stars and spotting clusters that look like a crocodile)
- History (the study of the great crocodiles of the past)
- Religion (tossing people into the Nile river and feeding the hungry crocodiles)

More subjects just meant more exams and crueller ways of testing children. I have no witty examples about Sharmaji or mammoths to share here. Timed written tests are not a joke.

800 Years Ago
England

Not satisfied with making the lives of young boys and girls miserable everywhere, adults opened universities and colleges all across the globe for other adults. And with these universities came a new type of exam: the university entrance exam. Already anxious parents became more anxious and children started preparing for these entrance exams at a younger and younger age. (We are now being taught topics in the Eighth grade that my parents studied in college! I say this is criminal behaviour.)

Writing equations was also no longer enough. One had to prove them as well. Old and dead Greeks were revived, and their ghosts still haunt us. Pythagoras. Need I say more? So, in a right-angled triangle the square of the hypotenuse is equal to the sum of the squares of the other two sides. Why do I need to know this? Why do I need to prove this? And why do I need to write a Latin phrase at the end of every proof? QED—what does it even mean?

When I become famous I am going to declare my birthday a holiday and call it QED—Quit Exams Day.

Present
India
Our ancient civilization has done more in the field of examinations than anyone else. Even our epics are about tests, assessments and competition. In the Mahabharata, Arjuna shooting an arrow at a fish in water while looking at its reflection in a mirror was giving a test. Hanuman, in the Ramayana, competed for the longest tail and the longest jump against all the other *vanaras*.

We pride ourselves on being the best test-takers in the world. But no more!

The tyranny of exams must stop!

We must fight against this drudgery!

Let us all submit our answer sheets right now and leave this classroom, never to return!

Let this essay become a beacon of hope for children everywhere.

Long live the resistance!

QED

Footnotes:

* Do you think this is some cutesy animated film set during the last ice age? When a mammoth gives you chase, you run. Don't try and climb a tree (the mammoth will pull it down). Don't run through an open field (mammoths run fast). Run uphill or hide in a small cave and then think about your life choices. What were you doing hanging around mammoths in the first place?

Trick questions and trick answers like these is why children hate multiple choice questions. Poking the mammoth will just make it angrier and bring about a swifter end to your existence.

@ The last ice age was brutal. Xi was lucky—he only lost one toe to frostbite. Li, after his encounter with the mammoth, lived on in infamy as children everywhere had to answer examination questions involving mammoths for the rest of eternity. How Li escaped the mammoth is a mystery lost to time. I have discussed various popular theories and conspiracies around this in my other essay titled, 'The Boy Who Ran with Mammoths'.

The Gorilla and the Girl

MENAKA RAMAN

'Humayun's Tomb is important for next week's midterm, students,' droned Ruby Ma'am.

Rukku was momentarily distracted by a dragonfly hovering lazily outside the classroom window. At the mention of midterm exams, her stomach went the other way, and fell.

'Midterms?' Rukku aka Rukmini squeaked. Uh-oh. Had she squeaked aloud?

Ruby Ma'am narrowed her beady eyes at Rukku, as the rest of the class started giggling and whispering.

Sri Manasarovar Matriculation Higher Secondary School, where Rukku studied in class 6C, had a rigorous and terrifying exam schedule. Everyone at school—from the Principal to the teachers to the parents to the students—took exams very seriously. If other people spoke about the weather, T20 scores and traffic woes, at Manasarovar everyone spoke about exams: setting exam papers (something teachers deviously relished), studying for exams, writing exams, correcting papers and discovering new ways to wheedle more marks out of teachers.

It was perfectly normal for parents to stand at the school gates after every exam, hands outstretched, waiting to snatch question papers from the hands of their children, screeching, 'Will you get centum?' 'Did Bernoulli's Theorem come?' 'Did you triple underline important points?'

Rukku found exams impossible. She could never remember things *exactly* the way the teachers wanted her to remember them. It seemed that only people with good memories and neat handwriting did well in exams. Plus, there were no exams on the things Rukku actually knew, like all 5,000 species of dragonflies, how to help a bird with a broken wing or how to feed beetroot curry (blech!) to your pet dog under the dining table without being caught.

It was only because her mother, Pushkala Ramaratnam, was the head of the Maths department at Manasarovar, that Rukku hadn't been asked to leave the school yet. But what would happen next week? Would Amma be able to save her again?

***

'Students. Keep your pencil box, geometry box and examination pad lined up in a straight line, neatly on your table where I can see them,' MPV Ilango barked. His actual name was Ilango Sir, but his love for talcum powder had earned him the nickname Mobile Powder Van or MPV Ilango.

Rukku yawned and did as she was told. She had stayed up way past her bedtime trying to remember the difference between LCM and HCF.

MPV looked up at the wall clock. *Tick. Tock. Tick. Tock.* When the seconds' hand finally crossed twelve and it was officially 9 a.m., he barked, 'Turn your question papers over.'

Rukku rubbed the orange-pink pebble in her uniform pocket three times for good luck before reading the first question.

Two chimpanzees are eating hot dogs. Chimp 1 has eaten 15 hot dogs and Chimp 2 has eaten 20. If a gorilla had to fight both the chimps for the hot dogs what would it use: nunchakus or the Pythagoras theorem?

Rukku giggled.

'I thought you'd appreciate the question,' said a deep, gruff voice.

Rukku let out a small scream. A giant gorilla was sitting next to her on the bench. He was easily six feet tall with a glossy coat of thick, black fur that turned grey on its back.

'You're a silverback,' Rukku said shakily.

The gorilla was slurping noisily from a delicately patterned china teacup, his pinky finger daintily pointing out.

'I believe that I am,' he replied.

'What are you drinking?' Rukku asked curiously.

'Matcha tea. The women in my troop say I need to lose weight,' snorted the gorilla.

'Sirrrrrrrrrrrrr!'

Rukku turned around. Class-topper Karthik, the insufferable know-it-all, was standing two rows behind her, his face the colour of jamuns.

'Sir. Questions are out of syllabus. We were not taught about primate Pythagoras theorem,' Karthik cried.

The silverback stood up, fixed his eyes on Karthik and beat his chest. Rukku felt the hairs on the back of her neck snap to attention, and she cowered. Karthik rightly took the gorilla's sign of aggression in the spirit it was intended and fainted.

'What a loser,' muttered the gorilla. 'So, are you going to solve this problem or not?'

'Me?' Rukku yelped.

'Yes, you,' the gorilla replied, pouring another shot of gross-looking green liquid from a teapot that matched the teacup perfectly.

MPV and the other students in the classroom were glued to their seats, staring at the gorilla with their mouths open.

'Umm...'

'To the blackboard. Go on. I don't have all day, you know.'

Rukku stood up on unsteady legs and wasn't quite sure how she walked to the front of the classroom. MPV managed to unglue his rear from his chair and stood up to face the gorilla.

'Ummm...Mr Gorilla Sir, Rukmani is not the best at problem solving. Perhaps we can ask Karthik once he wakes up to solve the sum? He is, after all, our class, school, state and country topper in IMO, NTSE, KVPY, HBBVS and...' MPV trailed off and mopped his powdered forehead when he saw the gorilla bear its teeth. 'Or perhaps we should just let Rukmini try.'

Rukku stood in front of the blackboard.

'Can ummm someone read the question out again?'

Mr Gorilla Sir pointed at P.V. Sumalatha, notorious for crying after all exams that she would fail, and then smugly scoring 99.9999.

'You. Read.'

Sumalatha stood up and held the sheet in front of her and read out the question, her voice ten times squeakier than usual.

'Two chimpanzees are eating hot dogs. Chimp 1 has eaten 15 hot dogs and Chimp 2 has eaten 20. If a gorilla had to fight both the chimps for the hot dogs what would it use: nunchakus or the Pythagoras theorem?'

The chalk screeched as Rukku dragged it down the board to write the first statement of the problem, muttering the words to herself.

'Number of hot dogs eaten by chimpanzee number 1...'

'Don't be tedious,' the gorilla sighed. 'You know you can't solve this problem like that.'

Rukku felt a small bead of sweat form on her upper lip. She wiped it away, closed her eyes, counted to three and opened them again.

Think, think, think! she told herself

'Umm...gorillas are primarily vegetarian and at the

most eat insects and termite larvae. So, it's unlikely the gorilla would want to eat the hot dog in the first place?' Rukku ventured uncertainly. 'Unless trained in captivity to do so.'

'Hmm...go on,' the gorilla said encouragingly, turning the teacup over and shaking out the last drops of tea into his mouth before chucking it over his shoulder. Students ducked to avoid the hurtling chinaware, as it went and crashed against the wall at the back.

'Also,' continued Rukku, wincing at the sound of shattering glass. 'If the gorilla did want to eat the hot dogs, it wouldn't use Pythagoras theorem or nunchakus. Gorillas are the largest known primates, and could easily fight the chimps, though they might consider it beneath their dignity to do so. They would probably show their dominance instead by beating their chests and screaming. Kind of how you just did with Karthik.'

'Excellent,' the gorilla nodded approvingly. 'Absolutely correct. Boy who fainted, read the next question.'

Karthik was getting up, swaying on his feet.

Heathen! Film not a whining Ada's
Stunning, freestyle lambada.

'Did you just roll your eyes at my question?' the gorilla growled.

'No! No! Th-th-there was a fly in it,' Karthik got back onto his wobbly knees.

'I thought as much. Okay child, answer the question.'

Rukku asked Karthik to repeat the question and

wrote it on the board. She stared at it for a while before writing the letters out in groups of small circles. The class watched in silent amazement as Rukku slashed at some letters, rubbed others out and placed them elsewhere, before writing out:

Silent, unseed, fading fast
Harming none, hated by all
What am I.

'Fart!' Rukku cried out in joy.

The entire class gasped in horror.

'Mr Gorilla Sir!' whined MPV. 'She doesn't mean th-'

'Sir! It's an anagram,' Rukku explained to MPV who had sweated all the powder off his face, leaving streaks of grey.

The gorilla got up off the bench and knuckle-walked to the front of the room.

'You're a smart girl, you know,' he said to Rukku 'and they aren't as smart as they seem. Remember that. Right, I'm off. You know how to call me the next time you're feeling down and out.'

'I do?'

'What's orange-pink, in your pocket and likes to be rubbed three times? Toodles.'

Rukku watched the gorilla amble out of the room. As he passed Karthik, he raised his fist. Karthik cowered in his seat, whimpering.

'Dude, fist bump?' the gorilla asked. 'No?'

'Wait!' Rukku called after the gorilla. 'How do I get out of whatever this is?'

'Look at your question paper.'

Rukku picked up the sheet and read the first question.

If a gorilla walks at 4 miles per hour, he covers a certain distance. If he walks at 9 miles per hour, he covers 7.5 miles more. How much distance did he actually cover?

When she looked up again, the gorilla was gone.

'What, looking here and there? Don't know the answers-a?' MPV sneered when he noticed Rukku looking around the room.

Rukku didn't feel the usual burn of shame on her cheeks. She smiled at MPV instead, bared her teeth a little in a gorilla-like fashion before she turned back to the paper and started writing.

Of Luck and Blue Fingers

DEVIKA RANGACHARI

When I was a child of five, I set out to write my first examination. I had been dispatched to bed very early the previous night so as to prepare me for the ordeal whose importance I only had a dim awareness of. All I knew was that I was to go to my sister's school on the morrow and answer some questions.

'And then you can come to the jungle gym and find me,' my sister told me that night and I nodded, thrilled at the prospect of an unknown treat, anxious about the lions and tigers that were bound to be at a jungle gym, and unbearably proud of my sister for negotiating the dangers of wildlife with such casual courage. If I thought about anything before I fell asleep, it was to wonder what school was all about and why animals were allowed to wander around it at will.

There is nothing more unnerving than finding anxious, parental faces hovering above you as you wake to greet the day but I took it in my stride, recalling, with a flash of joy, the jungle gym promise. I remember that my mother plaited my long hair with extra care and slipped a sugar cube into my hand as I left the house with my father.

In no time at all, I was at the school, seated in a huge, echoing room, at a scratched brown desk with a pencil, eraser and sheet of paper before me. I was in the middle of a long row that stretched right down the room with girls on either side.

'All right, children,' announced a lady who had walked in briskly. 'Are you all set?'

I remember nodding vigorously. I could hear yells and thuds from afar, and I wondered if we were near the jungle gym and if my sister was battling any animals.

'So you have to write numbers 1 to 15,' the lady said. 'You may begin now.'

I bent my head to the task and finished it quite quickly. Then I sat back, surveying the room and examining the interesting scratches on my desk. Everyone was still busy scribbling away. I wondered why they were taking so long. I desperately wanted to leave the room and find my sister and my consequent wriggling alerted the lady to my presence. She came and took my paper, and I was finally allowed to leave.

'Did it go well?' my father asked, worried.

'Yes,' I chirped. 'It was very easy.'

Much to my disappointment, I was shepherded straight to the car because we had to get back home.

To this day, I do not understand why the lady said

'15' when she actually meant '50'. As is obvious, I failed the entrance examination and was dispatched to a 'tent school'—one that did not have a permanent building but kept shifting locales as and where it pleased. I led a sort of nomadic educational existence in which every day began with trying to figure out where the authorities had seen fit to pitch their tent. By the time I rewrote the entrance examination and entered my sister's school, a year had elapsed and I was an older and wiser six-year-old who soon discovered, much to her discomfiture, that the jungle gym was a strange structure of intertwined bars and the idea was to hang from them so that the blood rushed to your head. There were no animals in sight except for the school dog, an ancient canine who slept his hours away and occasionally wagged his tail at the denizens of the school as a token of friendship.

My relationship with examinations grew odder and odder as the years progressed. There was the time when I wrote my heart out in a Hindi examination and then forgot to hand the paper in. I discovered it lurking at the bottom of my bag that night and resolved to give it in as soon as I entered school in the morning. However, when we drove up to the school gates the next day in a curtain of monsoon rain, it was to find that the building had been flooded and we were to return home forthwith. I spent that day with my heart sinking to lower and lower levels near my toes.

The next morning, the rain had ceased but my woes hadn't. The teacher refused to accept the paper as it had been lying with me for over forty-eight hours and so, I wasn't awarded any marks. To prevent such an incident from happening again, I pressed my friends into service. As a result, every examination that we took thereafter was marked by them staring at me, hawk-eyed, towards the end of the allotted time to ensure that I gave my papers in. Needless to say, it worked like a dream even if they didn't always finish their papers on time.

When I reached the Eighth grade, our studies suddenly became more complex. We were studying Economics for the first time in which you had to learn—and write—reams about the market and goods and other exciting things. Our first Economics examination was greeted with equal measures of apprehension and anticipation on our part, and we set to answer the questions as soon as we could. I wrote and I wrote but, for some inexplicable reason, the paper seemed never ending. I asked for endless continuation sheets but became suddenly aware that no one else seemed to be doing so and, in fact, a majority of them had laid down their pens. I wrote on, uncomfortably aware that everyone's gaze was on me and barely managed to finish the paper on time.

'So which of the questions did you choose?' asked the girl who was sitting next to me in the exam hall.

'Choose? There was a *choice* in the paper?' I realized then that in the 'long answer' section, we had to choose any three out of eight questions to answer and not having seen the instruction, I had somehow managed to answer *all* of them. My wrist ached for the entire week but what added insult to injury was that I was marked on the first three questions alone, which weren't necessarily the ones I knew best.

It was during this year at school that I realized, to my dismay, that my sight wasn't perfect. For long now, my parents had been warning me against reading, slumped in dark, cosy corners, and squinting at the pages of books while travelling to and from school. So one day I could read the blackboard perfectly; the next day, I couldn't. A Mathematics examination around the corner compounded my anxiety but I managed to cudgel my brains for a solution. My plan was to borrow my partner's spectacles at regular intervals to copy the sums written on the blackboard.

This would have worked brilliantly except that our partners were switched on that day to prevent cheating and I found myself sitting at the back of the classroom next to a cherubic girl from a junior class whose eyes gleamed with perfect vision. Resigned, I squinted fiercely at the blackboard. I managed to figure out the numbers written there through a combination of imagination and desperation, and began to solve the problems. I learnt later that I was solving sums pertaining to wholly different numbers altogether. And so, I failed the examination. My father's face when I told him what had transpired and why is a memory that I would prefer not to recall, at this point, or, indeed, at any point in the future.

It was when I reached the Tenth grade that

examinations took on a whole new meaning. Our Boards beckoned us with hateful smiles and we spent the entire year wishing them away but drawing inexorably closer to them. As this was the seniormost class in our school, we would have to leave and join other institutions, so it was crucial that we did well in our examinations. It was around this time that I discovered the power of my lucky pen. Whenever I wrote with it, the results were always gratifying. It seemed to me that my red, metallic pencil-box, on whose surface I had repeatedly etched my name with my compass, was equally lucky. So was my green eraser that nestled within a plastic case with 'Waikiki Beach' emblazoned on it.

I determined never to be parted from this triad. Wherever I went, these three magical objects went with me. On school holidays, I would arrange them neatly on my table and touch them lovingly to keep their luck flowing. And so, in this fashion, we reached the Boards. Our first ordeal was a Biology practical test where we had the choice of sketching a flying cockroach that was pinned to a wooden board or reproducing a flower that was our other specimen. It was while I was attempting to make a choice that my pencil-box flew off the desk, making a terrible din while crashing on to the floor. Everyone looked up, startled, and the invigilator glared at me.

I scrabbled around on the floor, making sure that the precious three were intact, and resumed my seat. But I was thoroughly shaken by the episode and the first thing I did was to pick up my microscope and look at the flying cockroach through it. The insect instantly became a giant and waved its feelers around, reminding me, in that awful moment, that it was merely chloroformed, not dead. I stared, transfixed with horror, through the lens until the scream that was gathering in my throat burst forth, and I flung my papers and lens away from me. I would not like to dwell on the aftermath.

The Chemistry practical test that followed was no better. Each of us was given an unknown substance in a little twist of white paper and told to discover its identity by conducting various experiments. I glanced at my lucky pencil-box and began to work. Fifteen minutes later, I was no wiser. My mysterious substance had tested positive for oxygen, carbon dioxide *and* hydrogen. I knew this was a physical impossibility unless, of course, an alien had flown down with a substance from its planet and substituted it for the one originally assigned to me. At this point, my pencil-box that had worked its way to the edge of the counter, all unknown to me, crashed on to the floor, startling me so much that I sent a vial of acid crashing to the floor, in turn, to keep it company. Some years ago, I visited my school and was overwhelmed with pride to note that I had left my mark on it quite literally. The white patch that had formed on the floor of the Chemistry laboratory that eventful day still remains.

My luck did not really change for the better, thereafter, despite my repeated and reproachful glances at the pencil-box and its contents. Take the History examination, for instance. We had two textbooks—one was world history; the other, Indian. There was a lot to prepare and learn, and I went for my examination feeling slightly dazed with all the facts swimming around in my head. The paper seemed terribly long but I persevered and just about managed to finish at the last moment.

'Which one did you do, Indian or the other?' asked my friend as we were walking out.

There was a choice? 'I did both,' I answered loftily.

She shrieked and broadcast the news to all and sundry, so that I was soon surrounded by the rest of the Tenth grade.

'You actually studied *both* books?' one of the girls gasped. 'But why? We were supposed to do only one!'

'I...I like History,' I said airily and tuned my back on them, thinking furiously. I *did* like History but not that much! I hadn't even known there was a choice!

Nevertheless, after this I was regarded with great respect, as having pulled off a near-impossible feat.

Even after I changed schools, I clung to my pencil-box and its contents even though the luck was clearly sporadic. Moreover, the pen was much the worse for wear with a distressing tendency to leak ink all over the place. To my friends and to all my examination invigilators thereafter, I was the girl with the blue fingers. The pen would splutter and choke and spray ink all over my answer sheets but perhaps the examiners found the resultant patterns artistic because I did manage to fare reasonably well.

When I returned to school with my friend many years later, I passed by a classroom where everyone was intent on answering some test or the other.

'Don't look in,' my friend urged me, 'or something weird will start to happen. The ceiling will cave in or everyone will fail or...'

'Ha! As if!' I retorted and began to walk on.

And then we both heard it—the sound of a pencil-box crashing to the floor.

I wonder now whether she was speaking the truth, after all.

The Bestie Test

DEEPA AGARWAL

We are the 3As—Apeksha, Anandi and me, Abhiri. We study at Wonder Woods School and are inseparable Besties.

Apeksha, whom we call A1, is medium sized, walks at a medium pace and never yells. She is A1 at Maths and Science, at all the subjects actually. She is also particular about eating healthy and tries to force us to live on salad like her.

'Where are your green vegetables?' she asks sternly every lunch break, after inspecting our unhealthy tiffin boxes. 'Ask your mother to send carrots instead of these oily fries.'

'But I hate carrots, they make me puke.' Anandi, aka A2, says stubbornly, puckering her mouth in distaste. Despite all the fries she devours, she is like a bamboo pole—tall and skinny and as springy. She has a LOUD voice.

'Compromise!' I—A3, usually step in at this point.

'Try a healthy tomato sandwich!' I mostly end up eating my boring, white bread sandwiches all by myself.

So, we 3As have disagreements, but are really, truly, inseparable. Even when we fight, it's only with each other—no one else.

It was A1 who came up with the Bestie Test. She likes to make rules and timetables. A2 and I let her, even though we're not very good at sticking to her rules and timetables.

One day, looking more serious than usual, she said: 'Friends should always stand by each other, shouldn't they?'

'Of course, don't we?' I replied, wondering what weird new idea had gripped her.

'I mean, we should swear a solemn oath that in any situation, the 3As will stand by each other,' she said. 'That will be the Bestie Test.'

'Awesome!' I was blown away.

'Don't we always stand by each other? We don't need a test for that. Unless it means you'll do my Maths homework?' A2's grin was broader than any emoji.

I couldn't help giggling. Though it struck me too, that we didn't need to test our friendship.

A1 frowned. 'Don't be silly!' she frowned. 'That's no test. If I do your homework, how will you learn anything? You'll end up failing in the exams.'

A2 snorted. 'What would be the Bestie Test, then?' she asked, curling her lips.

A1 looked mysterious. 'You will know,' she said quietly.

How? I wondered, not realizing that the test would come sooner than I could imagine.

The next day, at break, A2 and I were busy discussing plans for what our mothers still insisted on calling a 'play date' that weekend, when A1 interrupted sharply, 'Don't tell me that you've forgotten.' Her voice was high with disbelief. 'The half-yearly exams begin on the 21st. That's barely two weeks from now.'

Exams! I bit my lip. We *had* forgotten.

'They're only half-yearlies,' A2 mumbled. 'It doesn't mean we should stop having fun. And we'll meet only for a few hours on Saturday.'

'Count me out,' A1 said firmly.

'What? Please, A1!' I pleaded. 'You need some relaxation before the exams. And-and we can study a bit if you want.'

'Study? With the two of you?' A1 looked at us pityingly. 'Please Abhiri, why don't you grow up? You're eleven, you're in class 6, and our half-yearly exams begin in just over two weeks. It's insane to have a play date.'

She walked off, leaving the two of us gazing after her open mouthed.

This was just a starter to the terrible truth that burst upon us the very next day. When the bell rang for break, A1 informed us brusquely, 'I'm not coming to the playground. I-I want to stay here in class.'

'Stay in class? What for?' A2 gaped at her. 'Are you unwell? Shall we take you to the infirmary?'

A1 clicked her tongue exasperatedly. 'Can't you leave me alone? Give me some breathing space?'

We were speechless. Hurt too. Seeing A1's mouth set, I grabbed A2's arm and said, 'Let's go.'

'What's gone wrong with her?' A2 sounded almost tearful.

'I wish I could guess.' I shook my head, equally flabbergasted. 'But you know how she is. She must have made some weird timetable for herself.'

We hung around the playground gloomily munching our snacks. A2 didn't seem to enjoy her chocolate doughnut at all and I didn't even beg her for a bite.

A shrill voice startled us. 'Hmm, only the 2As today.' It was Punita, A1's chief rival for Best Scholar and there was a nasty smile on her face. 'The third A is studying so hard for her exams.'

We gasped. Studying? Why didn't I guess? But how much could twenty minutes extra study help? A1 was an achiever with a capital A, but this took the cake.

Before I could speak, A2 snapped, 'Any problem?'

'No, why should I have any problems?' Punita smirked. 'I'm not going nuts about my exams. I know I'll top and be Best Scholar.'

'Freak! Do you believe her?' I whispered, once Punita was out of earshot.

'Let's see for ourselves.' A2 frowned.

We tiptoed towards the classroom and peeped in cautiously. There was only one person there—A1, and what we saw stunned us. She had a book open in front of her and was repeating something in a monotone. It was her expression that scared us the most.

'This is insane,' A2 spluttered.

'What do we do?' I cried agitatedly.

'It's examination fever,' said a voice behind us. It was Atharva. 'You may not believe me, but it's a very serious problem. Hits high achievers. Ends up affecting their performance. You will need to intervene, if you want to save your friend.' He was the class Wikipedia, the boy with all the facts. But like Wikipedia, he could be misleading at times.

So, I shot back, 'What nonsense! She's always been very studious.'

He shrugged. The bell rang for the next period just then and A1 jumped in her seat like she'd got an electric shock.

What happened in the next period worried us even more. A1's hand was always the first to shoot up, whenever the teacher asked a question. Today she remained frozen, as if she hadn't heard. She kept tugging at her hair distractedly and I could have sworn that she was muttering to herself. She didn't even say bye to us when school was over.

A2 and I went home on the same bus. 'We have to do something,' I whispered, the moment I plonked myself into my seat.

A cryptic voice muttered from the back, 'I just looked it up on the Net. Hypnosis is a certain cure for examination fever.' It was Atharva again.

'Shut up!' I hissed. But a slight shiver shook me. Was something really wrong with A1? Everyone else seemed convinced there was.

'I'm only trying to help,' he replied with an injured look.

'Thanks!' A2 said sarcastically. 'If you have any experience in hypnotism do let us know.'

'Hmm...' His eyes gleamed speculatively. 'I-I'll let you know tomorrow. Just need to brush up a bit.'

'Look,' I said indignantly. 'I think we're overreacting. She'll be fine by tomorrow.'

'Fine.' Atharva shrugged.

A2 and I tried to discuss our weekend plans but our hearts were not in it and I was thankful when my stop arrived. And the following day, all the way to school, I kept praying that what I had hoped for would come true.

But it didn't. Once again at break time A1 waved us off, almost angrily, as if we were nuisances.

A2 couldn't control herself and cried out, 'What's wrong with you?'

'Nothing's wrong.' A1 replied. 'Now please go. Stop wasting my precious time.'

'All right, we'll go!' A2 snapped. 'But you're going nuts!'

'You shouldn't have said that,' I whispered, once we were in the corridor. 'Did you see her face?'

'Blank as a zombie's.' A2 ground her teeth.

'We have to do something.' I almost wrung my hands.

'What, hypnosis?' A2 grimaced. She fell silent as Punita loomed into view.

'One missing again,' she said sarcastically. 'I can't believe Apeksha's become that desperate. Tell her she shouldn't overload her brain. It's counterproductive.'

'Thanks for your kind advice.' I found myself snapping back. 'We don't need it.'

'You'll soon find out what your friend will need,' Punita replied, smiling maliciously. 'A doctor.'

We could only stare at her receding back.

'Hey! I was looking for you.' Atharva hurried towards us. He held up a keychain with a shiny medallion dangling from it. 'Watch!' He began to swing it in front of me. Without realizing what I was doing, I fixed my eyes on it...

'Stop! Stop! She doesn't need it!' A2's voice shattered my eardrums.

I blinked, then rubbed my eyes, confused.

'Worked, didn't it?' Atharva actually patted himself on the back. 'I told you.'

'Come then,' A2 said. 'It's almost time for class.' We hurried to the classroom.

A1 was bent over a textbook, muttering to herself. I sucked in my breath. This was even more serious than I thought.

A2 and I stayed out of sight, peeping through a window. Atharva strolled into the room. A1 didn't look up till he was standing right in front of her.

'Look!' He began to swing the keychain in front of her. 'Relax...relax...relax...'

A1's zombie expression got even more fixed. 'Relax...' Atharva droned on. A1 began to look drowsy.

'It's working!' I squeezed A2's hand. Just then, the bell rang.

A1 blinked. 'What are you doing, you fool!' she screamed so loudly that Atharva fled, terrified.

We could have screamed too, A2 and I.

Our play date was spent checking the Net for cures for examination fever. There were so many!

'What should we try? The herbal potion or the homeopathic pills?' I asked, biting my nails.

'It might be easier to get her to try the potion.' A2 tried to sound enthusiastic.

We had to first gather the ingredients. I didn't want to tell my mother why we wanted to make it, so I steeled myself and made up a story. 'We have a class project for herbal remedies,' I proclaimed brightly. 'Since a lot of us are worried about our exams, I thought we should prepare this.'

My mother examined me intently. 'Don't tell me you two are nervous? But you do look worried, Abhiri. It's so unlike you. There'll be plenty of time for examination fever when you get to your Board exams.'

I winced. Was there no getting away from those words?

Ma peered at the recipe. 'Hmm...most of the stuff's here in the kitchen...ashwagandha too? I have it. Someone recommended it when your grandmother had trouble sleeping.'

The decoction didn't smell too bad when it was ready. Thankfully, it didn't taste bad either. We poured it into a bottle carefully. If this didn't work, what else would?

On Monday, A2 and I planned our strategy en route to school.

The moment the bell rang for break, we hurried to A1's desk. 'I've told you to leave me alone.' Her voice was chilly.

'Okay, okay!' A2 held up a placating hand. 'We just wanted to share this health drink we made over the weekend. It tastes terrific.'

A1 clenched her teeth. 'All right. But just leave after that.' Gingerly, she took a sip from the bottle. Then she gestured to us to get lost.

We couldn't resist keeping watch through the window. To our delight, she kept taking swigs till she finished the whole bottle.

'Yay!' We gave each other triumphant high fives.

But our euphoria didn't last long. We kept an anxious eye on A1 for three days. Nothing changed. We might have just given her regular juice.

'Your friend really seems to have it bad,' Punita commented with fake sympathy, the third day. 'Try talking it out of her. Give her my example. Cool as a cat!'

I was searching for a really stinging response when that idiot Atharva butted in. 'Talk of bad...nothing short of an earthquake will affect her,' he said sourly.

Shut up! I was about to scream when a thought flashed through my mind. A2 seemed to have got the same brainwave too. 'Earthquake!' she yelled. 'Come on!'

We dashed to the classroom, hurriedly chalking up a plan. I took up my post near the window and began to rattle it, staying out of sight. A2 ran in yelling, 'Earthquake! Hurry! Get out!'

A1 groaned as if in pain. 'Leave me alone...can't you?'

'Look! Look at the window if you don't believe me.' A2 pointed.

Th next minute I rushed in shouting, 'Hurry! Hurry!' We grabbed A1's arms and ran out of the building, almost dragging her. At the entrance, we tumbled down the stairs and fell in a heap.

'Hey! Get further away from the building!' someone yelled. Atharva again.

I was giggling uncontrollably till several pairs of hands reached out to pull us up. And then I noticed the school buildings were actually swaying. OMG! Had we caused that earthquake?

Not possible...it had to be an uncanny coincidence. I clung to Anandi, shivering, as goosebumps sprouted all over my body. After a few moments she whispered, 'I-I think we passed the Bestie Test.'

'What test?' A1 rapped out sternly. My heart leapt to see her so normal again but both A2 and I couldn't speak for a moment.

Finally, I stammered, 'We-we wanted to jolt you out of-of—'

'Your examination fever,' A2 completed the sentence. She gulped. 'We...had to get you out of the classroom somehow. So, we pretended that there was an earthquake.'

Behind me Atharva proclaimed smugly, 'Don't forget it was my idea. The whole class thought you were going nuts, Apeksha. I was the one who said only an earthquake will cure her.'

'What?' A1 screamed. 'Even you two thought that?' She stared at us unbelievingly. 'You played this silly trick on me!'

'But A1, we were out of our minds with worry,' I protested.

'We had to bring you back to normal,' A2 added. 'Somehow, anyhow. Remember what you said? That in a sticky situation, the 3As will take any measure possible to save each other. That will be the Bestie Test? I think this was a very sticky situation.'

A1 was silent for a while. Then she took a deep breath. 'Thanks...' she whispered. 'I *was* going out of my mind. It *was* a sticky situation. You-you saved me.'

All three of us broke into smiles. The next day, the 3As were munching salad once again together in the playground, two reluctantly, one with relish. And the half-yearly exams? After this particular test, we just sailed through!

The Boy with Four Names

SHREEKUMAR VARMA

It was in Class Seven that Satwik Chandramouli Chandramohan Premachandran began to hate his name.

Until then, he thought it was an exciting name. He felt he was carrying his father and two grandfathers on his mighty shoulders. His father was Dr Premachandran, an eye doctor. Satwik's second name belonged to his mother's father, and the third to his father's father. Each time the teacher called out his name, they all seemed to stand up smartly with him and say, 'Yes, Miss!'

Satwik was known as The Boy with Four Names. In the class register, everyone else had initials, but his name ran on for three lines. His best friend S. Ram's name had only three letters, and one initial. Satwik felt sorry for him.

'No initials,' his father said firmly. 'A name is a name. Wear it proudly! Don't hide it behind stray letters.'

But one day, his class teacher gave him a shock. 'You know how much trouble I have writing down your name?' Mrs Karthik scowled at him. 'My fingers hurt by the time I finish!' Satwik stared back at her, which irritated her even more. She chuckled bitterly. 'Don't forget your mother and two grandmothers! Why don't you add their names as well? Then you'll sound like a radio jingle, or a laundry list! And it'll take six lines to write your name!'

The class burst out laughing. Satwik went red. No one had ever laughed at his impressive name. During lunch break, his friends joked about his name as if their teacher had set the ball rolling.

He came home and shouted: 'I don't want so many names!'

His mother was sitting at the dining table, writing a poem. She looked up with a puzzled expression. 'But you have only one, Satwik.'

'And what about those others? So many Chandrans in my name!' His mother smiled mildly and went back to work. 'Why should I carry other people's names?'

'That's *your* name, baba. You should be happy you have such a strong name.'

'Long, not strong!' He made a sour face. 'Mrs Karthik will cut my name, anyway. C.C.P. Satwik! That's what she'll write in the register.'

His mother smiled. 'Well, that's much easier to write, isn't it?' Her smile faded. 'I hope your father doesn't make a fuss about that.'

In school, his friends continued to tease him. 'See! See! Pee! Satwik!'

And even worse: his best friend S. Ram joined the gang. 'What a name!' he said, waving his arms. 'Chandramouli Chandramohan Premachandran Satwik! It's even bigger than the Indian Ocean!'

Satwik felt as if a pet dog had bitten him. 'Then you'll drown in it!' he snapped.

He ran to his mother. 'I don't like this school!' he cried. 'Why can't I just be Satwik? Why should I go around carrying everyone else's names!'

That night, he dreamt that his name grew bigger and bigger, coiling around him like a snake. He screamed and sat up in bed, streaming with sweat. 'It's too big! It's too big!' he gasped. When he went back to sleep, he dreamt he had pushed S. Ram into the Indian Ocean. When Ram started drowning, he woke up screaming.

He told his mother about the dreams.

His mother said, 'They say if you see two dreams, one of them will come true.'

Satwik grinned. 'Then I hope it's me pushing You-know-who into the sea!'

***

Mrs Karthik said the revision exam would be held next week. Tomorrow would be a holiday so they could study. Then she startled them with some terrible news: 'Grades from this exam will be added to the final exam, so don't even think of not studying!' Half the class said, 'Yaaay!' because of the holiday. Half the class groaned because of the sudden, unjust exam.

During the lunch break, there was a big buzz: 'I'll copy!' 'I'll study!' 'I'll simply write down the question paper!' 'I won't even have to study, I'll find it soooo-o easy!' 'I'll have stomach upset!'

'I'll skip it!' said Satwik. No one heard him in the general noise. He heard it, of course. His own words echoed in his ears: *I'll skip it...skip it...skip it!*

There was a big fat smile on Satwik's face.

Wow, that's a fabulous solution! I'll skip the exam!

He would hit two mangoes with one stone! Mango One: Two free days—the study holiday, and the day of the exam! Mango Two: The teacher would ask him for a leave letter for skipping the exam. Of course, his father would refuse to give such a letter. The teacher would complain to the headmaster, who'd throw him out of school. He would then join a better, more reasonable school! With better teachers and classmates! And a better best friend, he thought, as he dismissed S. Ram from his life forever.

***

Satwik didn't tell his parents about the exam or the study holiday. Next day, he walked out of home as if he was going to school. Idly swinging his schoolbag, he walked here and there.

There was a lot of traffic on the streets. He thought he'd never seen the city so crowded. He walked between tiny shops and big stores. He walked between cars, scooters, autorickshaws and cycles parked untidily on and off the pavement. The noise was deafening. He slipped into a side street, using his bag as a weapon to discourage people from bumping into him, and to punish those who did.

He thought he heard someone call him: 'See! See! Pee!' He turned pale. Had someone from school spotted him? Now he'd really be in trouble! It was one thing to plan how to be sent out of school. It was quite another to have his plan destroyed before it even began!

Satwik saw a small, smiling old man with thick spectacles. He sat in a box-like shop between an electricity transformer and a hand-pump. The board above him said: *Chakkiar's Frame Shop*. Satwik heaved a sigh of relief. This was a total stranger!

Now Satwik wasn't sure if he'd really heard what he thought he'd heard, but he glowered at the man all the same. The man wore a white *banian* and a *lungi*. Both looked dirty. Satwik had probably heard him wrong. He must have said something else.

'Hey, little boy!' the man said.

The shop was full of pictures, framed and unframed. There were pictures of gods and film stars; of nice places with trees, lakes and bright skies. Some pictures looked as if the artist had flung a few colours on the canvas because he had nothing else to do.

The man asked in a squeaky voice, 'Do you want a nice picture?'

'No!'

'Satwik?' Did he say that? *How does he know my name*! Did he actually say that! Or did he hear it that way? Satwik wasn't sure at all. It was a very noisy street. 'Framed or unframed?'

'I said I don't want a picture!'

The old man laughed. 'That's what you say! Don't you have a plan?'

'Plan! What plan?' stuttered Satwik. His heart was beating fast. Who was this random old fellow who seemed to know everything about him? How could he sit in the middle of the street and know things about people who walked by? 'I have no plan at all!' he snapped. He asked in a softer voice: 'Who are you?'

The old man waved him closer. 'That's not important. Many people will work miracles for you. You don't have to know who they are.'

'Miracles! What miracles?'

The old man peered at Satwik. His eyes were enormous behind his spectacles. Satwik looked at the man's face with its untidy silver beard and large hump of a nose. He looked at his bright smile, showing some teeth and some places where there used to be teeth.

'What miracles?' he asked, feeling stupid.

'I can give you a painting,' said the old man.

'I don't have money.'

'That's no problem. Pay me when you can.' He began to pull out various paintings, both framed and unframed. 'What is your name?'

Satwik set his mouth in a defiant line. 'Satwik Chandramouli Chandramohan Premachandran,' he said forcefully.

The old man studied his face. 'I thought so!' he said. 'Someone like you needs something like this.'

'Like what?'

The man grinned. 'I have just the thing for you.' He rummaged some more in his shop, and came up with a framed painting. It looked like something scrawled by a small child. 'Can you tell me what this is?'

'It's a picture of the sea,' said Satwik, peering closely. 'And that big black thing in front is a big whale.'

The man shook his head. 'No, little fellow, it's not!'

'Yes, it is! It's the Indian Ocean.'

'It's a big field actually. And that thing in front is a big black bull. Take it with you and everything will be fine.'

Satwik snorted. 'I don't like it!'

The old man laughed. 'You don't have to like it to make it work!'

'Make what work?' asked Satwik.

'Your miracle.'

Satwik snorted again. 'This stupid picture is my miracle?'

The old man removed his glasses, closed his eyes and smiled a mysterious smile. 'You won't know till you can know that it can be, will you?'

That left him confused and silent. The shopkeeper laughed and pushed the painting at him. The old man was so persistent that Satwik took the painting from him.

***

Satwik took the painting to school, wrapped in newspaper.

Many of the students were already sitting in the hall, waiting for the question paper. Mrs Karthik looked important and very busy, as she usually did on exam days. Satwik flung his bag on the pile of other bags and walked into the hall, holding the painting.

'What are you bringing inside the exam hall!' cried Mrs Karthik. 'Don't you know you're not allowed to...?'

Satwik smiled at her. 'For you, Miss,' he said sweetly.

Mrs Karthik rolled her eyes. 'This is an exam hall! Don't you know you're not allowed to...?'

Satwik tore open the newspaper and threw it away. He pushed the painting into her hands. 'Gift for you, Miss,' he said.

'How can you bring me a gift during exams!' Her voice crackled with surprise and anger. 'Don't you know you're not allowed to...?' She seemed to be stuck with that one sentence.

But the painting was already in her hands. She stood there, glaring at Satwik, and not knowing what to do with the painting. There was an excited chatter among Satwik's classmates.

'How dare you, Satwik Chandramouli Chandramohan Premachandran!' Mrs Karthik shouted.

No sooner had she uttered his long, unwieldy name than a deep tremble shook the hall. To everyone's shock, the painting began to flow out of its frame. First, it was drop by drop, but then it soon grew into a trickle. Mrs Karthik peered suspiciously at it. Then water tumbled out like a waterfall from the canvas. 'It's not a field!' yelled Satwik triumphantly. 'I told him it's the Indian Ocean!'

It roared and it poured. It flooded the floor of the hall, and charged at the students who screamed and jumped up on their chairs.

Mrs Karthik fell back as the canvas shot up to the ceiling. She heard a scream from somewhere near her: 'What is my name? What is my name?'

Mrs Karthik screamed back: 'Satwik! Satwik!' Children and teacher began to float. Soon everyone in the room was swimming, sometimes here, sometimes there. 'I like it!' screamed Mrs Karthik. 'I like your name so much, Satwik Chandramouli Chandramohan Premachandran!'

The water rose and rose. As the painting sailed away from the room, Satwik shouted and swam after it. He heard a crazy scream and saw S. Ram being chased by an enormous black whale. Satwik left the painting and swam furiously to rescue his best friend.

***

Satwik felt a terrible pain in his left ear.

He looked up to see the old shopkeeper sitting in his box-shop, laughing uncontrollably. 'What a boy you are! What a boy you are!' he said through his laughter.

'Let go of my ear!' yelled Satwik.

'That's not me,' the shopkeeper laughed. 'That's your father!'

Satwik gasped. 'My father!'

He twisted his neck to look up at the man who was grimly holding on to his ear as if he would never let it go. It wasn't his father! 'You, boy!' came the thundering voice of his school headmaster. 'What are you doing out here on the street, boy? In uniform, and carrying your schoolbag!' He screwed up his eyes. 'You're the boy with four names! Don't you have an exam today?'

Satwik felt terribly confused. 'But the school is flooded,' he cried. 'We can't go in.'

The headmaster looked down at the dry pavement. He looked up at the clear sky. He saw the people and cars, the scooters and cycles. 'Flood!' he said in a voice that sounded like a tiger's growl. 'Does this look like a flood to you, boy?'

It took several more minutes of the headmaster's lecture and the shopkeeper's laughter to bring our Satwik back to dry earth and the terrifying thought of today's exam.

The Exam Ghost

LAVANYA KARTHIK

'Quick! What's the answer to this one?'

'Thirteenfoursarefiftytwo, thirteenfivesare...eesh! I forgot!'

'...and if I pass, God, I promise I'll eat palak everyday and say prayers and...'

I made my way through the crowded corridor, listening to the sounds of last minute revisions, eleventh hour memorizing and desperate pleas for divine help. There was a nervous hum in the air, a crackle of excitement, a dull throb of fear. I could feel it too, bubbling up in my stomach, tingling in the tips of my fingers, tightening in my throat and thudding in my brain. It was the day of class 6B's Maths exam.

I hovered at the edge of a group of boys and girls from my class, listening to them mumbling formulae and chanting multiplication tables. Then I joined another group, competing for the 'who has studied the least' prize. I rolled my eyes. They were all class toppers, who did little more than study all day, and revise all night. You know the kind, I'm sure, the sort who'll say 'Haw! I didn't study only! I'm going to fail!' and then pretend to be very surprised when the results are announced and they've topped. Not like me at all.

Then something caught my eye at the far end of the corridor. Away from the crowd, two boys crouched by the wall outside the Physics laboratory, peering at something on the wooden panelling that lined the lower half of the wall. Their books and pencil-boxes lay strewn around the floor. I knew that corner well. And I knew those boys—Freddie from the back row of my class, and the new boy, Adnan.

'It's the exam ghost! I swear! That's his name, scratched into the wood there!' Freddie squeaked in excitement.

I groaned. Every year, for as long as I'd been in this school, I'd heard the story of the exam ghost being narrated to some wide-eyed student or the other. No one ever seemed to know the real story, no one told it like it really was. I doubted Freddie would either. Still, I headed over and hunkered down beside them.

'Uff! It's so cold.' Adnan straightened up and folded his arms around himself.

'Cold!' Freddie scoffed. 'In Mumbai? In March? What planet are you from?'

'Haha. Now, what am I supposed to look at?'

'Arrey, there! Right in front of your big nose!'

'That?' Adnan peered closer, his nose almost squashed into the wood. 'It says "Pee-vee-cee-vee-i-bee".'

I leaned over to see for myself. It did say that.

'Not vee-I, Adnan, you dodo! That's a six in Roman numerals. 6B...our class!'

'PVC?' Adnan scoffed. 'What, was he made of plastic?'

'Dumbo!' Freddie hissed. 'Those are his initials. His name was Pacha...picha...something.'

I frowned. Couldn't he even get the basic details straight? But I said nothing.

'So, what happened to him?'

'He was this boy in 6B and he was really afraid of Maths.'

'I hate Maths.' Adnan's face scrunched up. He looked worried. Maybe his stomach was fizzing and bubbling like mine did before the exam.

'I also.' Freddie sat very still. Was he thinking about the paper ahead, I wondered. About the paper and, if he was anything like me, about the way the numbers would never, ever behave like they were supposed to. About the way they just danced around on the page, and muddled up things inside his head and left him feeling confused and dizzy and foolish. And about how even the simplest sums wouldn't add up like they were supposed to, as if they were teasing him, like mean kids on the playground. And all the while, time was ticking by and his teacher was frowning at him, and his dad was expecting 'Good marks, sonny boy, at least this time!' and his mother was sighing and making him go to tuition, and...

'So this Pichapucha...' Freddie's voice snapped my

brain back out of its dizzy spin. I felt the fizzing and bubbling and tingling and jiggling all over me gradually die down. 'Are you listening?'

Adnan bit his lip as he watched his classmates pace up and down muttering things, tracing sums in the air. Then, he turned back to Freddie.

'So...what happened?'

'Okay. This Pachapecha didn't just hate Maths, he was afraid of it.'

'You mean, scared of the teacher? Probably some *rakshas*, like our Mr Faleiro.'

'I swear, such a devil he is!'

'Ya, bet he has a forked stick in his hand, like Satan. To poke students in the bum, heheheh.'

'Bet he has a forked tail also, hohohoho.'

'Bet he has horns also, under his wig!'

I watched as Adnan and Freddie rolled around for a bit, sniggering and bumping fists. Down the corridor, the burble of last minute revising grew louder; the panic in the air, thicker.

'So,' Adnan said, wiping his eyes with the end of his tie. 'What happened to Kichapicha?'

'Pachapucha. No, wait...Pachapicha.'

'Machupichu! Heheheh!'

'Oho!'

'Tichukichu! Hahahah!' Adnan was clearly on a roll.

'Forget it then!' Freddie huffed.

'Ya, ok, ok. Tell fast!'

'Ya, so...he'd start shaking like a jelly before every exam. His hands would jiggle, his knees would jiggle, his tummy would...'

'Figgle, hehehe.'

'You want the story or not?'

The first bell rang, making us all jump. And reminding us we had ten minutes before the exam began. Adnan glanced down at his books, suddenly nervous, then turned back to Freddie.

'Then?'

'So, I was saying...This boy would get really scared before the Maths exam. And he would shake and shiver and all. And then one day, when he was in sixth grade, on the day of his final Maths exam, he got so scared, so scared, he...'

'He what?'

'He...'

'Wha—aat?'

'He...shook so hard, he...' Freddie opened his eyes wide, in mock horror. He was enjoying this, I could see. He had all of our attention, and he was going to milk it for all it was worth. He stopped, frowned, closed his eyes and shook his head.

Adnan's mouth was as wide open as his eyes. He leaned in. So did I.

'You're right, it is cold,' Freddie said, rubbing the goosebumps on his arm.

'Uff! Don't change the topic! What happened?'

Freddie lowered his voice. His eyes narrowed. A grim expression took hold of his face as he scanned the small space we were crouched in. He swivelled around to look straight at me, turned the other way, then turned back to Adnan.

'Pachapucha got so scared of the Maths exam, he started shaking. And he couldn't stop. He shook and he shook and he shook!'

'And?'

'And he shook and he shook and he shook!'

'Ya, okay! Then?'

'Then he shook and he shook and he...OUCH!'

I had to laugh. Adnan had grabbed a textbook and swatted Freddie across the head with it.

'Duffer!' Freddie grabbed his textbook back and aimed at Adnan. THWACK!

'Dodo!' Adnan returned with another blow. THWACK! He grinned.

'Mothball!' Freddie swung his book again. THWACK! He grinned back.

'Dungbeetle!' THWACK! THWACK!

I watched as they duelled with their tattered books, all three of us giggling like babies. I sighed. This was fun but time was ticking and I really wanted to hear how the story ended before the exam began. I sighed again, heavier this time.

The books on the floor rustled and flapped as if caught in a sudden breeze. The two warriors stopped, a little startled. I watched a pencil roll out of Adnan's Chota Bheem pencil-box and across the floor. Finish the story, I thought. Another pencil joined it. The books on the floor fluttered faster.

'It's going to rain, maybe?' Adnan said, reaching for the runaway pencil.

'Looks like,' said Freddie, fiddling with his books.

Behind them, the sun shone brightly on the other side of the window.

They gathered their books and pencils and made for the classroom.

I hurried behind them, hoping to hear the end of the story.

We were nearly at the end of the corridor, near the rest of our classmates. Freddie waved an imaginary book at Adnan, who laughed and waved his right back.

'So, scared?' Freddie asked.

'Yes,' Adnan said. 'But not so much. Not like before.'

'Me too. Not so much.'

I grinned. I felt better too. For the first time in all these years, I really did feel better on Maths exam day.

'It's just an exam,' Adnan said, but without much conviction.

'Tell that to my dad,' Freddie smiled. 'And my tuition sir.'

'And my Ammi.'

'And Mr Faleiro with his bum-poking fork.'

'Hahaha. And Kuchukicha.'

'Pachapucha. Oi, I didn't finish!'

The second bell rang. Two minutes till the exam. The other students began milling around us, still chattering, still waving their books about.

'You didn't! What happened...and don't say he shook again!'

'Heheh...you should have seen your face, but.'

'Don't start. Telling or what?'

'Okay. That Pachapucha shook so much, so much...'
Adnan waved an imaginary textbook.

'...he just disappeared.'

'What!'

'I swear! He just, like, evaporated or something.'

'No way!'

'Yes way. Some people say he shook so hard all his cells came loose and floated into the air and merged into the walls.'

'Whoa!'

'And some people—well, mostly my older brother, okay. He passed out of Tenth standard last year. He says Pachapucha's cells are still here in the air and the walls and on the curtains. And every year, on the day 6B has its final Maths paper, they magically come together and merge back into Pachapucha. Or rather, his ghost.'

'And he eats people and curses them and stuff, right?'

'What? No, he doesn't hurt anyone. Why would he? My brother says the ghost just floats around, watching everyone prepare for the exam, then goes back to being atoms till the next year.'

'Oh. So he can't, like, move cupboards and bathtubs across the floor and stuff.'

'He's an exam ghost. Not Agrawal Movers and Packers.'

That's true, I thought. But he can move things, small things. Like books and pencils. Didn't Freddie know that by now?

'Oh,' Freddie added. 'And whenever he passes by, you can feel a chill breeze.'

'We felt a chill breeze!' Adnan gasped.

They stared at each other for a moment. Freddie swivelled around, looking for someone who looked like they were made of magically fused atoms. I almost did too.

'Probably just a breeze,' he finally said.

'Probably.'

We lined up outside 6B.

Mr Faleiro loomed in the doorway of 6B, glaring down at us. He seemed to be on a snack break; in one hand he held a plate of fruit, in the other, a fork.

'Come on, get to your...what are you two boys laughing about?'

From a corner of the class, I watched the students of 6B settle down and start their exam. I watched the smart ones smile and dive for their pencils, and I watched others who weren't quite so eager. And I watched Freddie and Adnan read through their question papers, grimace, then catch each other's eye across the room. Freddie made a face, Adnan made another; they grinned and waved imaginary books at each other. Then, giving each other a little thumbs up, they started on their papers. I smiled; I was going to miss them. But something told me they would pass and move out of 6B. I was never going to see them again.

I only wished I could have told them that almost every word of their story was true. That the exam ghost was really once a boy in 6B and, once a year, still is.

That he did fear Maths and that his cells really do live on in the walls of the school. But most of all, I wished I could tell them that his name wasn't Pachapucha or Kichakuchi or Macchupicchu.

My name is Pachamuthu Veerapandian Chockalingam, and I was once afraid of Maths.

Lakshmi Perumal's New Label

C.G. SALAMANDER

Alchemists and sorcerers have spent centuries looking for the fabled philosopher's stone—a stone so powerful that it can cure diseases, turn lead into gold, and grant its finder immortal powers. It was the promise of these unimaginable powers that led the modern-day alchemists of India to band together and form Alchemy Bhavan, an organization dedicated to finding and recruiting the best alchemists across the country.

You see, the philosopher's stone wasn't really a stone to begin with, instead it was a chemical substance that was yet to be discovered. Legend has it that only the most disciplined practitioner of alchemy could decode and fully comprehend the ancient recipe needed to create the philosopher's stone. The alchemist in question needed to be an expert chemist, needed to have a steady hand, and should know the valencies of every element on the periodic table by heart. The elders of Alchemy Bhavan had been on the lookout for such a person for decades; they searched the country's many chemistry societies, they ransacked the labs of the IITs, and they even went so far as to check if the Indian Space Research Organization (ISRO) had any alchemists on their payroll. After spending decades of resources and millions of rupees, Alchemy Bhavan was finally convinced that they'd found the perfect alchemist—a brooding Chemistry professor named Maha Rao who was rumoured to possess an intellect that rivalled Einstein himself.

The society of alchemists presented the professor with a state-of-the-art laboratory, they shared the ancient book of alchemy for him to decode, and they provided him all the compounds and materials he needed to run successful experiments. Professor Rao was thrilled to be recruited by the society. Finding the philosopher's stone was what he lived for, and now he had all the resources to make his dream come true.

Professor Maha Rao stood close to his glass cauldron, toiled day and night, refusing to eat and sleep. The professor followed the instructions in his book to the letter, and invested all his energy in creating the philosopher's stone. Then one day Maha Rao took a deep breath—he was approaching the end of his experiment. All that was left was for the liquid in his test tube to turn green. The tired professor lifted the volatile, bubbling green test tube cautiously—one drop too many would blow up the lab, and a drop less would freeze it into an iceland. Rao steadied his hand, concentrated hard, and when the moment was right, he added the bubbling green liquid to the glass cauldron.

Nothing happened.

Professor Rao grinned nervously at the elders watching him from a glass room. He began sweating profusely, rummaged through his formulae, rechecked his calculations, and tested and retested his equipment. The professor tried his best to ignore the impatient elders of Alchemy Bhavan. He paced around his lab restlessly—nothing made sense anymore. He had followed the recipe to the letter, he'd completed his experiment with perfection, and yet he'd failed to create the philosopher's stone. Maha Rao knew that this could only mean one thing, someone else must have beat him to it. Someone else must have perfected the formula.

I need to find that person, Maha Rao muttered to himself.

Professor Rao rushed back to his lab and toiled for hours together. This time he built a strange device, one that looked a lot like a glowing taser. Then he packed his bags and ventured out of his lab that evening, sure he'd find the philosopher's stone.

The elders of Alchemy Bhavan saw Maha Rao holding a strange device when he left their facility. They were convinced that Rao would find them the philosopher's stone. This was Alchemy Bhavan's sixth attempt to find the philosopher's stone, and they were surer than ever that they were going to find it.

Inside the confines of Maha Rao's skull, he was filled with a deep longing for the stone. He felt that the stone was rightfully his, after all he'd worked so hard for it, and everyone was counting on him to find it. The professor pointed his device at a tiny school on top of a hill and chuckled. He began walking towards the school. He was bent on tracking down the genius who'd successfully created the philosopher's stone, and once he was within arm's reach of them, he'd steal the stone for himself. Or better yet, the recipe.

***

St Fritsi's Matriculation and Higher Secondary School sat on top of a tiny hill in a sleepy suburb in Kodaikanal. Anyone who saw the school from a distance imagined it having a picnic all by itself. The school was surrounded by patches of carrots and cabbage, and was blanketed by a sheet of green moss. Wildflowers grew on the walls, the roof was a vibrant shade of red, and the children who studied there wore bright green uniforms with even brighter green berets—in short, St Fritsi's school looked like something that belonged in a fairy tale. But despite the overall prettiness of the school, there was one part of the building that looked dilapidated and run down.

Everyone from St Fritsi's feared the crumbling Chemistry lab located at the far end of the primary school building. The walls that connected the Chemistry lab to the rest of the school were severed on purpose, and the lab was the only part of the school that was bereft of grass or flowers. The walls of the lab were ash grey, and the clay tiles on the roof looked singed and oven baked. No one from St Fritsi's dared enter the Chemistry lab, especially not when *she* was around. Teachers, parents and children feared her equally, and they all dreaded the Chemistry periods. Teachers would show up to the lab wearing protective cricket pads and helmets. Parents prayed for their children, and handed them tiny black-and-white pictures of Marie Curie, Louis Pasteur and Michael Faraday with the hope that the famous chemists would keep them safe. The lab was no place for a child, especially not when Lakshmi Perumal was around.

Lakshmi Perumal of class 6C was the reason the Chemistry practical exam had been postponed five times. At first glance Lakshmi Perumal looked harmless, she was a little over four feet tall, and wore pigtails coiled around a thin iron rod that held up her hair and made the pigtails point slightly above her beret on both sides. When it came to most of her subjects, Lakshmi was an above average student eager to learn her lessons. But there was something about Chemistry that brought out the worst in her. Being the curious child that she was, she would often run amok around the classroom, mixing chemicals together at random.

The children from her class claimed that during her previous practical exam, Lakshmi had charged into the lab and mixed beakers of chemicals that were stocked away in the highest shelf of the lab. Many of the children present on that fateful day confirm that Lakshmi had added a bubbling green liquid to a concoction of salts. They claim that the reaction had been so violent that it caused an explosion so large that it singed and darkened the red clay tiles on the roof. But if that wasn't unbelievable enough, the children also claimed that their poor teacher was caught in the explosion, and that Lakshmi was somehow unaffected by it. The children swore that the chemical reaction had given birth to a glowing yellow stone, and they swore they saw Lakshmi pick it up and place it under her beret. But when they were asked about the whereabouts of their Chemistry teacher, they simply shook their heads mournfully, claiming that he'd vanished into thin air.

The children's stories, however, weren't taken seriously. The principal simply laughed at their tall tales, and remarked that his students had fairy-tale imaginations to go along with their fairy-tale school. The principal sent the children who'd gathered to raise their concerns about Lakshmi out of his room, and ushered in the new Chemistry teacher, a brooding old man named Maha Rao.

'It's like I said, Maha Rao sir, just conduct and finish this practical exam successfully, and I'll make your place in my school permanent.'

Professor Maha Rao nodded. Then he made straight for the men's washroom. He grinned maniacally into the mirror and pulled out the taser-like device from his coat pocket. The device was beeping louder and faster than ever. He was sure he was at the right place.

***

Inside the Chemistry lab, Lakshmi Perumal waited eagerly for her new Chemistry teacher. Today was the day she was finally going to pass her practical exam.

Lakshmi heard footsteps and watched the other children in her class stand up. 'Good morning sir!' Lakshmi joined in. But while the other children sat down, Lakshmi ran to the front of the class to meet her new teacher.

'Good morning sir, my name is Lakshmi Perumal, and Chemistry is my favourite subject!' She exclaimed excitedly.

'Good good,' Maha Rao smiled, and then heard a siren-like alarm go off inside his briefcase.

'What's that sound, sir?' Lakshmi asked curiously.

'This, err...this is nothing,' the professor stalled, reaching into his bag to fish out his taser-like device. Maha Rao glanced at the reading on the device, it was off the charts.

'What is that, sir?' Lakshmi asked once again.

Maha Rao didn't reply, he was too busy inspecting the reading on his device. The professor pointed the device at the class, and when he moved it towards Lakshmi, he dropped the device and winced in pain. 'The device has overheated itself,' Maha Rao whispered to himself, 'she must be the genius.' He scratched his head, confused.

'Iiiii! Light is coming, sir!' Lakshmi exclaimed once more, and picked up the device from the floor. But the moment she touched the device, it sparked and emitted a cloud of metal-coloured smoke.

The children from Lakshmi Perumal's class exchanged looks with each other, they knew this wasn't going to end well.

'I'm sorry sir, it was already broken when I touched it,' Lakshmi grinned apologetically.

Professor Maha Rao looked at Lakshmi and then at his device. There's no doubt about it, she must have the stone, he thought to himself.

'That's alright Lakshmi, it was a silly device to begin with,' he forced a smile, 'you can go back to your place and we'll start the exam.'

Professor Maha Rao studied the classroom, he was certain that it was Lakshmi who had discovered the philosopher's stone, but he had to make sure.

'Okay children, I want you to begin this exam by doing exactly what you did in your previous exam.'

'Even me, sir?' Lakshmi hesitated.

Professor Maha Rao stood in front of Lakshmi's table. 'Yes, you too Lakshmi,' he smiled, placing his hand on her head.

Lakshmi looked unsure. 'Are you absolutely sure, sir?' she asked again.

'Of course, child,' Maho Rao began.

Lakshmi picked up a bottle of dilute sulphuric acid from the shelf. 'You're sure no, sir?'

'For the last time Lakshmi, I'm positively sure!' Maha Rao smiled violently.

Lakshmi watched the beaker in her hand slip and crash to the ground. The sulphuric acid gushed out and splashed near the professor's leg.

'Aiyooooooo!' Maha Rao howled in pain. 'Why did you spill acid on me?' He winced, hopping around on one foot and wailing in pain.

'But sir, you told me to begin by doing exactly what I did last time,' Lakshmi protested, 'and I began the last exam by accidentally spilling some sulphuric acid on the teacher.'

'I meant the—' words struggled to leave the professor's lips, he felt like crying, he felt like swearing at the top of his voice, but the professor refrained from doing so.

'Don't worry about me, luckily it was just dilute sulphuric acid,' he tried not to grunt and groan while he spoke, 'so please do carry on.' He leaned closer towards Lakshmi. 'What are you waiting for, Lakshmi? Do what you did last time!' he said.

'Sir, you shouldn't be leaning in so close,' Lakshmi Perumal interrupted. 'The Chemistry book says it isn't safe.'

'I'm a professor of Chemistry! I'm one of the greatest chemists in the world!' Maha Rao scoffed, 'So rest assured that I know what I'm doing, child.' There was something about the way he used the world child, it was almost as though he'd meant it as an insult.

'You're the teacher, sir,' Lakshmi shrugged and turned on the Bunsen burner.

The professor watched Lakshmi closely, he saw

her reach for the chemicals on the top shelf, and he watched her mix a couple of salts together.

Professor Maha Rao sniffed the air. 'Do you smell that?' He asked no one in particular. 'It's a sort of burning smell,' he began, 'which one of you foolish children burnt your experiment?' Maha Rao asked firmly.

'I think it's your tie, sir, it's been burning for the past two minutes, and I think it's about to reach the nylon bit soon!'

Professor Maha Rao looked down and was alarmed to find a raging fire working its way up to his collar. 'Quick! Give me something!' Maha Rao cried frantically, reaching towards Lakshmi.

Lakshmi was caught in the process of mixing two beakers of chemicals. She held a blue liquid in one hand and a colourless liquid in the other. Lakshmi thought long and hard about which beaker to hand over, and eventually passed along the one with the colourless liquid.

Maha Rao, who'd grown suspicious of the little girl, avoided the beaker with the colourless liquid and snatched the beaker with the blue liquid from her hand. He poured it liberally over his tie and the fire momentarily went out, but a couple of seconds later it burned stronger and brighter than before.

'Arrrrgggghhhhhh!' The professor exclaimed.

'Are you sure you're a Chemistry teacher, sir?' Lakshmi asked, concerned. 'Why would you willingly choose kerosene over water to put out a fire?'

Professor Maha Rao didn't respond to Lakshmi's question, he was too busy removing his shirt and rolling on the floor to put out the fire.

That's it, I give up, Maha Rao thought to himself, but then he glanced at Lakshmi and to his surprise he found the girl holding up a test tube with a bubbling green liquid. It was the very same liquid he had synthesized in his lab a few days ago. But unlike his test tube, Lakshmi's solution wasn't nearly as violent—it was calm and stable. 'That's it!' The professor exclaimed, 'That's the final step!' His eyes shrunk with madness. He had figured out how he was going to get the philosopher's stone.

'I don't care about your stone anymore,' he pronounced loudly, 'I'm going to destroy you and your stone along with it, and then I'll be free to create my own philosopher's stone!' He began to chuckle maniacally.

The children in the classroom looked at each other, and without speaking a word they ran outside the classroom.

'Add one extra drop and you'll explode! Add a drop too little and you'll freeze!' The professor hummed cheerfully. He waited for Lakshmi to begin pouring the bubbling green liquid into the beaker, and pounced on her the moment the green liquid touched the beaker.

The sound of a large explosion resonated across the empty corridors of St Fritsi's School. 'Oh great, she's done it again,' sighed the Twelfth standard class teacher from the opposite side of the school building;

the teacher paused for a couple of seconds and after the sound of the explosion subsided she went back to her Maths problem on the blackboard.

Lakshmi stood at the centre of the classroom. She crouched down and picked up a tiny stone the size of a glowing yellow marble. Then Lakshmi Perumal removed her beret and placed it on the ground. Inside her beret were five more glowing yellow marbles, and they all looked different from each other. Lakshmi took the marble in her hand and dropped it into her hat along with the other marbles. The little girl sighed, 'I guess the exam has to be postponed again,' she said to herself, 'but at least I found another marble,' she smiled to herself and skipped on home.

'I hate Chemistry.' One of the children standing outside finally broke the long silence.

The other children nodded their heads in agreement.

***

A week later, the principal held yet another inquiry. 'I'm going to ask one last time!' the principal demanded, 'What happened inside the classroom?'

'The Chemistry teacher, and then Lakshmi, there was a loud boom, and then...' The children spoke all at once.

'One at a time!' The principal thundered.

'It's the same as what happened the past five times!' One of the children exclaimed. 'The new Chemistry teacher insisted that Lakshmi do exactly what she did in her last practical exam, and like the others, he went into a fit of madness when he saw the bubbling green liquid. He said something about a stone belonging to him, and then he tried to push Lakshmi when she mixed the green liquid into a beaker. That caused an explosion so large that it made the teacher disappear. We saw Lakshmi engulfed in a roaring flame, and still nothing happened to her, it was as though she was immortal!'

'An explosion made the Chemistry teacher disappear?' the principal scoffed. 'Lakshmi Perumal is a disruptive student, and she's chased away yet another Chemistry teacher,' the principal said firmly. 'I won't have you spreading this nonsense about stones and vanishing explosions.'

The children fell silent.

***

Back at home, Lakshmi was busy polishing her yellow marbles. She took them out of her beret carefully and placed them on her desk. She polished the stones patiently, and when she was done shining them, she placed them on the matchbox beds that she'd made for them.

Right next to the matchbox beds were five broken taser-like devices piled one on top of the other. Lakshmi reached for her backpack and dug out the sixth one. She inspected the broken device for a couple of seconds, and after giving it some thought, she stuck a label on the device and kept it with the pile of tasers.

She placed a taser-like device in front of each of the matchbox beds. And on the labels of the various broken tasers were names that were either suffixed with the words sir or ma'am. Lakshmi placed the sixth device in front of the stone she'd most recently acquired—it had the words 'Maha Rao sir' labelled on its side.

Final Itch

CHATURA RAO

The itch in the seat of his pants began to bother Golu three days before the first Final Exams of his life.

Golu was eleven years old and in the Sixth standard at RPS, or Raj Public School, a famous boarding school in the hills.

It was early March, still cold in north India, so the itch could have been caused by winter dryness. Golu didn't really know. His mother was too far away to check and tell him what might be causing this tickly feeling that ran along the edges of the elastic of his underwear when he was sitting, and in circles over his bums when he was walking around.

Golu ignored the itch for the most part because he was terribly worried about the Final Exams. The mid-terms in September last year had been a disaster. He'd tried to study like the rest of the kids, but when faced with the question papers, had forgotten most of what he'd read. He'd broken into a cold sweat at the start of each exam, fretted about flunking while trying to answer questions and had, sadly, failed in two subjects.

Now he didn't think it would help to study for the Final Exams. He hated the long hours of study. Today, they extended from 5.30 p.m. to 8 p.m. in the grand old school library. Here the Sixth and Seventh grade students sat with their heads bent over their books, with only the scratch of pens or the rustle of pages turning, to break the silence. Golu was bored, anxious and hungry. He felt like he was trapped in the temple of a ruthless Exam God, who hurled textbooks at him from the high, ornate ceiling like bolts of lightning... bolts that he tried to dodge.

So he told Miss Miriam, the teacher in charge of watching them, that his stomach hurt. He was in luck! Miss Miriam, usually suspicious, excused him from Study Hour. Golu went back to his dorm room. He gleefully ate a bar of chocolate from his tuck box— the box of goodies that he had brought back from his vacation at home—and huddled happily under his blanket.

But the fear of the exams followed him into his dreams where letters scuttled off pages and chased him like ravenous crabs down the corridors, while his classmates sat at their desks writing answers that got them straight A's.

The exams added a flavour of misery to the already-horrid experience of living far away from his PSP and his mother, in a boarding school. Golu's Ma had come to meet him last month with gulab jamuns, his favourite sweet. She'd doled the syrupy sweets into a little silver plate as soon as they had seated themselves in the Visitors Room. Golu had begun popping them into his mouth, dribbling syrup down his chin, which she'd lovingly mopped with tissues.

'How's school?' she had asked when he took a break after his fourth gulab jamun.

'Still awful, Ma!' Golu had whined.

'It hasn't even been a year yet, beta,' she'd cajoled.

'I'd even get used to jail if you left me there long enough!' he grumbled as he popped another gulab jamun into his mouth. 'You know, Ma, everyone compares me to Daddu here! They say I can't really be his great-grandson, since I'm so bad at things.'

'But you are *good* at things...' Ma said, pushing a lock of hair off his forehead.

'Like what?' Golu stopped slurping, to ask.

'Like... like... eating,' she offered.

'I try my best at studies and sports,' he said, sadly shaking his head to the seventh (and last) gulab jamun in the box. 'But Ma, Daddu was such a great student and athlete that he makes me look bad!'

Golu's Daddu or great-grandfather, Shri Prakhar Singh, had been a famous student of RPS. While still in school, he had grown to a height of six feet five inches. School records showed that he had excelled at sports and had been the school topper. So imagine what Golu had to face...

If he came to class with homework sums done

wrong, the Maths teacher would shake his head, 'Three wrong answers! Your grandfather was a cent-per-cent student. Why can't you do better?' If Golu scored a goal in a football match, the coach would say, 'Just *one* goal? Your grandfather always scored at least five! Looks like the genius gene levels ran low by the time you came along!'

Now the tickly-itch that was bothering Golu made Shri Prakhar even more detestable to him. Here's why.

Golu could not scratch his bottom in front of his mates. They'd laugh at him. Which meant that he couldn't scratch at all, except in the washroom, and when he'd head there...

'Go meet Dadduuu!' the other kids would jeer.

For, on the wall opposite the row of sinks, inside the boys' loo, was a huge tiled portrait of Shri Prakhar. It had been a long-held wish of Shri Prakhar to renovate the plumbing and general decor of his old school's washrooms. His Trust had recently fulfilled this wish, on the condition that his portrait adorn the wall of the boys' washroom.

Golu stood there, scratching, with handsome Daddu staring down at him, and he compared their figures. Daddu had been as muscular as Golu was, well, gol-matol or of rounded form. One of the family's favourite stories was of the time when Shri Prakhar, at the age of eighty, had wanted to show his strength by carrying one-year-old Golu on his shoulders 12 kilometres up a mountain. Only, Golu had been so upset at being separated from his mother that he'd attacked the old man from upon his shoulders, pulling a tuft of his luxuriant hair out by its roots. Shri Prakhar had worn a turban from that day on, until the day he died.

The portrait on the loo wall showed Shri Prakhar with his turban on. Golu was glad he'd had a good go at Daddu, who was casting such a long and terrible shadow on his present school life!

Lying in his bed the night before his Final Exams, Golu fretted and fumed, 'Couldn't Daddu have been less awesome at everything? Wherever he is, I hope what's left of his hair falls out!'

His tears glistened in the light of the moon that shone through the window on the row of beds. Except for the snores of sleeping boys and the single, sad bleat of a goat in the meadow outside, the dorm was quiet. Golu too drifted off to sleep.

The next day, the dreaded Final Exams began. Seventy kids shuffled down the curving wooden staircase to the exam hall on the ground floor. They passed maharajas and freedom fighters in ornate frames that lined the yellow walls of this 200-year-old school building.

Most of the students had their books out for a last-minute cram. Today was History. They walked in two's and three's, recounting the reasons for the decline of the Indus Valley Civilization and explaining the main points of Jainism and Buddhism to each other. Golu walked alone, awkwardly. Terror at the prospect of facing the question paper made his bottom tingle and itch more than ever.

He sat at the desk allotted to him among the rows of desks in the hall that accommodated the Sixth, Seventh and Eighth graders. First the school prayer was played over the PA system, during which time the kids either sang along, or muttered prayers of their own. Golu prayed for a miracle. 'I wish I could be eating tufts of grass, like the goats and cows, at the border of the hockey field. I wish I could be anywhere but here!'

The Sixth standard question papers were distributed by Miss Miriam, her eyes sharp behind her black-framed glasses. Like little x-ray scanners, they surveyed the room. She hauled up a few Seventh graders whose pen-cases and pockets yielded cheat slips. The Sixth, that was writing their first final exams, shrank nervously before her.

Golu read the first question.

List three similarities between Buddhism and Jainism.

He thought hard but nothing came. Except, from his bottom, the tickly sensation rose up his spine and continued along his left shoulder. Golu ignored it. He scribbled on his answer sheet—

Three similarities between Buddhist and Jainist:

1. Both have bald monkes

2. Both have 'ist'

3. I don't know

P.S: Dear teacher, I hope you give me a mark for my hones—

Suddenly he saw a line moving along his arm—ants! Before he could shake them off or squash them they'd descended along his fingers and onto his answer paper. They formed the words—*No, Golu beta*

They continued to quickly form the lines:

They began in the 6th century BCE

They were reform movements

Both preached non-violence

Golu was so shocked, his mouth dropped open. The pen fell from his fingers. The ants scrambled to the far corner of the desk.

Clumsy boy! It's Daddu, here to help you. Copy down the answers quick.

Golu looked for Miss Miriam. She was sitting at her desk at the head of the hall and x-raying the boys in the front rows. Safe. Phew.

He copied the answers as they appeared on his desk, as quickly as he could. All the while his mind raced. 'OMG! The itch was a bunch of ants with a message *from the dead.*' His heart lifted like a parachute in the wind. He was proud to be the heir to such an accomplished man—one who could direct ants into answers, and move Golu's academic score from zeroic to heroic!

'With Daddu on my team, I'll never have to study for an exam again!' Golu imagined himself grown-up and dancing at a party while his classmates slaved over their books. He saw himself winning a gold medal at the Indian Foreign Services academy while they sat looking on sadly.

When he finished the last answer, Golu set his pen down and flexed his tired fingers.

Meet me at the Memorial, the ants formed, then.

'Mem...what?' Golu whispered. 'Uh, the loo?'

What a crude word for a shrine to my memory, the ants quivered.

Golu looked blankly back.

Right. The loo. Meet me there.

The ants whizzed up Golu's arm and into his sleeve just as Miss Miriam came to collect the answer sheet.

After the exam, when everyone was in the lunch hall, Golu sneaked into the boys' washroom. He stood before Daddu's imposing tile portrait, his plump knees knocking in excitement.

'Pranaam, Daddu,' he folded his hands. The portrait was as stoic as ever. There was a grey-brown, snot-shaped stain on the tile right below his grand nostril.

'Thank you so much for sending your ants to my rescue.'

'Me-ehh?' was the reply. It came from one of the cubicles. Golu looked around, startled.

'Me-ehh. In here.'

Excited and nervous, Golu pushed open the door of the cubicle. It was empty. But then, he spotted a face. A huge goat with a hairy chin and distinctly bald pate had pushed his face through the window slats and was peering at him.

'D... Daddu?'

The billy goat chewed on a tuft of grass that was hanging out of the side of his mouth. Daddu, Golu recalled, was often to be found with a cigar dangling from his lips. He could see the resemblance. The light-coloured, unblinking eyes, proud flaring nostrils and the patch on his pate which Golu had been responsible for weeding on the mountain trip ten years ago.

'They owed me one,' the goat grunted.

'Who?' Golu asked, puzzled.

'The ants. I'd carried them away on my back when the pest control people fumigated the school kitchens, thereby saving their lives. So I got them to return the favour by making answers for you in your exam. But that's it. Never again, young fellow. You've got to answer the question paper on your own tomorrow.'

'B...but...'

'I'm the goat. I butt. You're the student. Study!' The vision Golu had seen of himself, all grown-up and partying before a big exam, swished down the nearest toilet.

'STUDY? What a harsh goat you are, Daddu!' Golu cried, stung. 'You've made my life hard enough by being such a big shot in school!'

'I was not a big shot,' the goat bleated. 'I just loved being at RPS. The teachers were great, the food was tasty, the green campus and playing fields were fabulous. So I worked hard. I loved it so much, I asked to be reborn right on this campus!'

He chewed contentedly, while Golu thought about what he'd said.

'So you were not a real genius?' he asked.

'No,' Daddu replied. 'Stop worrying about matching up to me. Try enjoying yourself instead.'

'Hmm, I can try,' Golu nodded, thinking of the lunch laid out in the dining hall. RPS did still serve delicious food.

'I'll try studying for tomorrow's exam and see how I

do. Bye, Daddu. I'll come and meet you by the hockey field sometime. Thank you for letting me know there was no genius gene in our family after all.'

'Bye, puttar,' the goat replied affectionately to his great-grandson. He withdrew his huge head from the window slats.

Golu left the loo, whistling. He didn't notice the last of the ants streaming down his trouser leg and leaving the building through a vent in the floor. He felt awesome. He had met his great-grandfather, who was not an annoying super-achiever, but a nice goat after all.

Plus, his bottom didn't itch any more.

The Magician Who Had a Cold

NANDINI NAYAR

Long ago, Magician Vedraj's Magic School had the reputation of being the best Magic School in the Kingdom of the South and was famous for teaching practical magic. It was at this time that a girl named Laali came to the school.

Laali was a thin girl with anxious eyes and pulled back plaits that gave her face a pinched hungry look. The Kingdom of the South had just gone to war with the Kingdom of the North. The fields lay waste, and a dull dusty haze hung over them. All the men and women had been taken away to fight the war and there was no one to grow vegetables or tend to fruits. Laali's village lay close to the border, where food was scarce and this explained her constantly hungry look.

Laali's father had sent off his daughter hoping he would see her come back a trained magician. Her mother, far more practical, had said, 'At least Laali will be fed well at the Magic School!'

And for the first few months at the Magic School, Laali *was* fed well. Vedraj had his own healthy, growing fields that supplied the wants of the school. Then one morning, Vedraj appeared at the breakfast table with shocking news. 'As you all know,' he said, 'the war has damaged the soil of our country and our fields don't produce as much as they used to. And now, hungry villagers have begun to steal from our fields and gardens!' A murmur of outrage ran around the table and Vedraj said, 'We understand that they are hungry, but...'

What he meant was that there would be less food for the children. The pale pinched look returned to Laali's face. Perhaps it was being constantly hungry that brought on a cold so she went around with a red nose, sneezing mightily. For such a small person, everyone agreed, Laali had a very large sneeze. People stayed away, afraid of catching her cold and Laali talked to her friends through notes or by shouting things from a safe distance. And then, to add to the misery, Vedraj declared that they would have their year-end exam.

Because this was a Magic School, they would be practical exams. The other students went into huddles, discussing formulas and quizzing each other. But poor Laali had to study by herself, with only her cold for company.

On the day of the exam she went into the large laboratory, heart thumping uncomfortably. Her head was thumping too and together with the thumping heart, it made her feel as if she was having a small, private earthquake. It was going to be a long day, and Laali knew her brain would have to be flexed and unflexed several times. She drew in a deep breath and walked to her work table.

A mango seed lay on the table, hairy and hard. It was as big as a football and the students had to first shrink it and then hide it in a tray of mud. For the first time in days, Laali smiled because she knew how to do this. She was humming as she began making the formula—a rusty humming with sudden thick snorts as all the gooey stuff in her nose interfered. Nobody knew what she was humming; all they knew was that it was a *happy* humming.

And when Laali stepped back from her pot of deep brown formula, she was smiling. It was perfect; the right thickness to shrink the seed to a tiny size. The brown was the exact shade of mud and would hide anything dipped in it.

And so, Laali grabbed the mango seed in a pair of tongs and dipped it. She looked at the clock and began to count the seconds. According to the formula, the seed had to be dipped for exactly twenty-four seconds in the liquid.

At the tenth second Laali felt something beginning to slide about in her nose. At the fifteenth second she knew there was no escape. She needed her handkerchief or the snot would be out! At the seventeenth second, she reached with her left hand into her right-hand pocket and pulled out her handkerchief. A loud honk on the handkerchief cleared her nose. Relieved, Laali looked at her seed and felt her heart sink. For the seed, in all this twisting about for the handkerchief, was no longer dipped in the formula. It hung suspended over the pot, brown drops dripping off its long hair. Oh no, Laali thought. She splashed the seed back into her formula and held it there.

Her heart was thudding fearfully when she pulled it out at the twenty-fourth second. What would she find? She found the seed, tiny as a small pea. She was squinting at it doubtfully when someone said, 'That's a really small mango seed.'

It was Magician Vedraj, nodding encouragingly and saying, 'Bury it in the soil and we'll see what happens!'

Laali buried it and they stood back, watching the soil.

'Should be coming now,' Vedraj was saying, when something shot out of the soil at a tremendous speed. Laali leapt back as it whooshed past her, rushing for the roof.

Around the laboratory, work stilled as everyone turned to see what Laali's seed was doing.

'It's growing,' Laali said unnecessarily. The seed was now a tree, with lofty branches spreading widely under the roof of the laboratory.

'Yes, yes,' Vedraj nodded. 'I wonder... '

A minute later there was a sudden thick wet thump and a squashed ripe mango lay on the laboratory floor.

'Mangoes,' Vedraj said happily. 'Lovely, lovely!'

And yes, the branches were laden with golden yellow fruits and the rich smell of ripe mangoes filled the room.

'If you've all finished the first question,' Vedraj said, 'let's enjoy some mangoes!'

'But...what about the examination?' Laali stammered.

'Examinations come and go,' Magician Vedraj said. 'But ripe mangoes come only once a year! Let's enjoy them.'

Who would have imagined, Laali thought, that they would have a mango-eating break during an *examination*? But Magician Vedraj seemed to think it was necessary and by the time they had all eaten their fill of mangoes, they were glad he had suggested it. The mango tree was carried away to be planted in the garden, with Magician Vedraj following, to ensure it was done properly. He came back smiling hugely.

'It's a miracle,' he told Laali. 'That tree grows fresh mangoes every two seconds. How did you time it that way?'

Laali shrugged but her heart thumped with the secret of her knowledge. *Two* seconds! The exact time that her seed had dangled *out* of the brown liquid. What if the Magician found out? He would be sure to fail her for her carelessness.

Laali moved on to the second question, determined to be more careful. This asked for the formula to clean vessels. Laali measured and mixed the chemicals carefully, glad her cold was finally under control. She wasn't sniffing and the heavy feeling in her head had vanished. Had she accidently created a medicine to get rid of colds?

She bent over her formula, sniffing anxiously. The strong smell went up her nose, tickling madly and instantly, her cold was back.

She sneezed hugely and people turned to look at her. 'Do you want to rest?' Magician Vedraj asked anxiously.

How could she rest with one more question left to finish? Fortunately, it was an easy question, asking for the formula to clean vegetables. They had done this several times and Vedraj had explained how this formula could help their countrymen.

'A large percentage of vegetables are wasted because they are spotted, soft or because they have worms,' he had said. 'This formula can rid the vegetables of these and increase the food available!' It was easy to see that Vedraj was proud of this invention. He had a reason to be proud, Laali thought, looking at the potato she had to clean. It was a medium-sized one with four large spots on it, spreading damply across the brown skin.

'Poor Miss Potato,' Laali sighed. 'If I chop you now, you'll be a tiny potato by the time I get rid of the spots!' The potato seemed to shrink with shame, looking small and pathetic.

'Don't worry, Miss Potato,' Laali comforted it. 'Once I dip you in Magician Vedraj's amazing Vegetable Cleaning formula, you'll be beautiful!' Miss Potato seemed to perk up at her words and stopped looking so sorry for herself.

Laali mixed the chemicals, measuring carefully, pouring cautiously and all the time, explaining the steps to the potato.

'There,' she said lighting the stove under the pot. 'This has to boil for ten minutes. And this time I am *not* going to lose count of even one second!'

Miss Potato seemed to approve. Laali watched the clock as the chemicals boiled and when nine minutes had passed, she said, 'Almost done! Very soon now, Miss Potato, you'll have a makeover!'

She measured out the last ingredient, saying, 'Ten drops of this, that's all this formula needs!'

She held the spoon, ready to drop it into the formula. And that was when Laali felt a sneeze coming on. Her eyes widened as the sneeze came rushing down her nose, tickling and taunting her. 'Oh no,' she said, looking around wildly for help. But everyone was busy and anyway there was no time for the sneeze was at the door, tickling madly, refusing to be held back. And then **ATTTTICHOOOOOOOO**, it burst out of Laali's nose and mouth, spraying snot, and squeezing her eyes shut. It shook her from top to toe and the spoon in her hand jumped madly about. The liquid in it spattered into the pot and the formula there hissed at once.

When Laali opened her eyes, the formula was a hissing green and the spoon in her hand was empty.

'Did I make a mistake?' she whispered to Miss Potato. But Miss Potato was no help at all, maintaining a dignified silence.

'Only five minutes to go,' Magician Vedraj called.

'What shall I do?' Laali asked Miss Potato. But Miss Potato simply stared back at her, her brown spots making her look ill and weak. They reminded Laali of her promise to Miss Potato.

She picked up the potato with the tongs. 'Ready?' she asked and then plunged the potato into the green fluid. She held it there for five seconds and then pulled it out.

The skin of the potato was smooth and brown. Laali stared at it, hardly able to believe her eyes. 'I did it,' she whispered. 'I did it!'

The bath in the formula seemed to have done Miss Potato good. She looked healthy. In fact, thought Laali, she seemed to be bursting with health. This was when Laali made a horrifying discovery. 'Miss Potato,' she gasped, 'you are growing bigger!'

By the time Miss Potato stopped growing, she was as big as a large pumpkin and everyone in the room was standing around Laali's table watching her. Magician Vedraj was there too, beaming as he told Laali, 'Wonderful! Amazing! Can you imagine how many people that one potato will feed?'

Laali tried to smile but in her head her cold thumped about viciously. Her heart was thumping too. Miss Potato might feed many people but Laali had made a mistake. What if she failed the exam?

But Magician Vedraj was too happy to do anything like that.

'Magic is not the blind following of formulas,'

he told Laali. 'It is the practical application of knowledge!'

Of course Laali was happy. What made her even happier was that she was allowed to keep Miss Potato. She sat on a special cushion in Laali's room, reminding her every day of the real purpose of knowledge and the endless uses it could be put to.

The Happy Birthday Exam Song

ANDALEEB WAJID

I was a cheater. I had cheated in my exam. It was written all over my face. I knew it and I knew the people I passed by on the road could read it, loud and clear. My body felt hot and cold at the same time. Why had I done it?

It wasn't like I had planned to copy during our first-term Chemistry exam. I just felt like I had crammed so much in my head that all the information would slip out if I so much as sneezed.

I literally believed that and walked gingerly to class that day, hoping my head could hold all the information I had force-fed into it the previous day and this morning, right until it was time for the exam to begin.

But two things happened that changed everything. My friend Kamya ran up to me the moment she saw me and started chattering non-stop about how she had forgotten everything she had studied. She was jumpy and excited and nervous and it rubbed off on me and I felt that familiar anxiety grip my stomach.

I didn't even nod because I was afraid of all the chemical equations falling out through my ears but it had all already started floating around perilously like hydrogen because it was...because it was...I had no idea about the properties of hydrogen.

My eyes went wide and I quickly retrieved my Chemistry textbook from my schoolbag and flipped the pages to the chapter on hydrogen. But just then this annoying girl called Lekha, who constantly liked to sing songs, entered the classroom. She was singing a song I had never heard before. The weird lyrics got lodged into my head instantly, displacing all the Chemistry equations and formulae I had stored carefully.

Suddenly, all my brain wanted to do was sing 'Hawww...tera happy birthday, hawww tera happy birthday!'. WHAT? No no no. Brain, get back in control. Put everything back in its place, I told it furiously. But it was too late. My brain had decided that it liked this idiotic song and promptly learned the entire lyrics that began with something like, 'Main, meri girlfriend, tu, tera ex, sab milke gayenge happy birthday'.

Now what could I do? I gulped and looked around and quickly tried to push the song out but it had sunk its tentacles into my brain and wouldn't move. Just then the bell rang loud and clear, in that shivering way it does and everyone was either rushing out or rushing in from the classroom.

I sat down at my desk, all the time feeling like throwing up. Thank God I had not eaten a heavy breakfast though Mom kept trying to make me eat a sandwich at least. I had grabbed a glass of milk and downed it but now thanks to all the acid my stomach was secreting, I knew it had all become a curdled mess. This much Chemistry was all I could remember.

As I sat there nursing my curdling stomach and exploding brain, Chaya came and sat next to me. I frowned. This wasn't her seat. We'd been assigned seats according to our roll numbers and mine was right up in front. Chaya was at least five seats behind me. I looked around. The class had been rearranged today, even though it was the last exam.

I shrugged. No use wondering about that when I was trying hard to recall the properties of hydrogen and all my brain wanted to do was sing 'Tera happy birthday'.

Mrs Venkat passed around the question papers and I looked at the white sheet in dismay. I had known the answers to these questions just this morning. But my brain was rebelling and my stomach was churning.

I started writing but no words came out. I took a deep breath and as I exhaled, I glanced at Chaya who was neatly answering the questions on her answer sheet. She was a sweet girl and also the class topper. She was the kind of girl who never suspected anyone of having any mean thoughts about her, and she didn't even bother covering her answer paper as she wrote.

Mrs Venkat was monitoring the classroom but she

was strolling around the last benches because that's where most of the copying happened. Everyone knew of her sharp eagle eyes and no one dared try and copy when she was monitoring an exam. But she hardly ever ventured to the first half of the class.

After ten minutes of singing the happy birthday song in my head, I was on the verge of tears. But I didn't want to be *that* girl who fainted or made a fuss and I controlled myself. Maybe there was a way I could salvage this situation, I thought.

I sat up straight and breathed in carefully and looked to my right to Chaya. Before she turned the page, I had to do something. So carefully, I rubbed my eyes as though something had got into them and edged closer to her. I read the first answer and tried to put it down verbatim in my answer sheet. I couldn't obviously do that for all the questions but maybe I'd be able to copy just enough to pass the exam.

Right at the end, with about five minutes for the bell to ring, I went over my pitiful answer sheet. It was ridiculous. I had barely answered even half the questions. That's when I realized that the song was no longer playing in my head. Eyes wide, I quickly put pen to paper and started scribbling away furiously as answers magically popped up in my brain, back in their place after they had kicked out that stupid song.

But the bell rang too soon and Mrs Venkat took away my answer sheet mid-scrawl. I looked at her, almost explaining what had happened to me, but kept my mouth shut. She collected all the papers and went back to the desk. I had messed up totally.

Everyone looked relieved and excited because the exams were over and the Dasara holidays were due to begin but before they could celebrate, Mrs Venkat cleared her throat.

'Class, it has come to my notice that there has been a lot of cheating going on in these exams. That's why we switched the seats today,' she said, and looked kindly at Chaya who smiled back at her, clueless that quite a few girls had most likely copied from her. I looked down guiltily, once more 'Tera happy birthday' playing in my head. I flashed an angry look at Lekha who was staring at the ceiling dreamily. Her lips were moving and I was sure she was singing another song. I looked away immediately.

'So, we are going to be very strict in our corrections. If anyone is found having written the exact same phrase as anyone else, we're going to pull them up,' Mrs Venkat said with a grim smile. I stared back at her, shocked.

'But...'

'How...'

'There are definitions...'

The class erupted in loud protests. Mrs Venkat nodded calmly and then shook her head. I didn't know what she meant. Yes or no? To what?

'Don't worry. I know what to look for and what not to look for. I just wanted to warn you all that the correction for this exam is going to be super strict. We are going to make sure none of you ever decides to copy again,' she said. 'Oh, and happy holidays!'

I looked at my classmates and knew that not everyone who looked worried was guilty of cheating. They were probably genuinely worried that they might be accused falsely. And here I was. I had cheated today, and I felt the weight of it crush me down like those heavy pianos that fall on top of cartoon characters, flattening them completely. I only wished I could peel myself off the floor and walk away.

On the road, I avoided making eye contact with anyone. I felt like there was a huge placard floating above my head with 'I am a cheater' written in screaming capitals. I was half afraid Mrs Venkat would pounce on me from behind a bush and say 'Aha!' By the time I reached home, I was faint with nervousness.

I rang the doorbell nervously. What if the school had found out already and had called Mom to inform that I was a cheater?

But when she opened the door, she looked excited and that flummoxed me further.

'Surprise! We're going to Darjeeling!' she announced.

What? Why? How?

The questions were plain on my face and she quickly explained as I walked inside. Apparently, she and Dad had been feeling bad about how much I was slogging for these exams and had quietly planned a vacation when I had been least expecting it.

'When are we leaving?' I asked Mom, dropping my bag on the floor. My exam board slid out, a horrid reminder of what I'd done and I shoved it back inside the bag quickly.

'Tomorrow morning!' she said. What? But I hadn't packed or anything. She caught the look on my face and shook her head.

'It won't take long,' she said as she led me inside. That was when she remembered the exam.

'Accha, how was your exam?' she asked. I felt my throat seize and close up completely. I couldn't talk so I just shrugged.

She sighed and shook her head. 'How many times have I told you to make an effort, Anandita,' she said sadly. I didn't reply to her because I was honestly worried at how much more disappointed they were going to be with me when the truth came out.

But until then, there were these two weeks of delicious holidays and I intended to have as much fun as I could. However, the weirdest thing about vacations is that they get over before we can really sink our teeth into them and enjoy them.

Before I knew it, we had gone and come back from Darjeeling and it was already time for me to return to school. Oh how I dreaded the beginning of the second term. It was such a boring beginning because there was none of the excitement of new classrooms, new books, new desks and maybe new faces too.

'I loved all your vacation photos on Instagram!' Kamya squealed when she saw me. I rolled my eyes but grinned back at her. Then I saw Mrs Venkat walk into the classroom holding her register and my excitement fled. She was not only our class teacher but our Chemistry teacher, too.

I sat down at my usual place and looked around for Chaya. Where was she? Ah. There she was, in the second row looking at Mrs Venkat with a smile on her face. I wondered what went on in Chaya's mind. Was her internal chatter anything like mine? I doubted it.

Mrs Venkat took attendance and then looked over at us over the edge of her spectacles. Fear flooded my stomach and I felt it fall all the way down. What was going to happen? Was she going to demean the girls who had cheated? Was this going to be our punishment?

She cleared her throat and I sat straighter. 'I'm very disappointed, girls. You're in Ninth standard. This is not how the almost Tenth standard students perform,' she said.

I looked at her steadily but instead of denouncing all the cheaters, she went and sat behind her desk and pulled out several answer sheets from a voluminous bag that she had kept near the desk. My stomach sank to the heels of my shoes now. Inside that bag was the answer sheet I had copied from Chaya!

'I'll be calling you, one by one,' she said softly, fixing her glasses firmly on the bridge of her nose. So it wasn't going to be public humiliation but privately she was going to destroy us, I thought. One by one, the girls went to her as she called out their names randomly. No one knew when their turn would come.

'Chaya!' she called out. Chaya got up and returned in just two minutes, her eyes wide and shocked.

'Anandita!' she called out. I sat up startled. The walk

to Mrs Venkat's desk suddenly seemed very long. I reached Chaya's desk and saw her answer paper. She had got 45/50 and she looked devastated. I wanted to roll my eyes at her but Mrs Venkat was waiting for me.

'What is this gibberish, Anandita?' she asked as she glanced at my paper.

'I...' I didn't know how to defend myself.

'The first half of your answer sheet made no sense, Anandita,' she said softly. Huh? The first part meaning what I had copied from Chaya?

'So I decided to score you on the second half of the answer sheet,' she said. She looked at me almost kindly and I wondered if she had discovered that I had copied from Chaya. Wasn't she going to punish me?

'Don't do it again,' she said softly as she handed me my paper. Obviously, I had failed but I wasn't too worried about that. I looked at my answer sheet and flipped the pages and saw that she had given me full marks for each answer that I wrote at the end of the exam, which I hadn't copied from Chaya.

'You're a good student. Whatever happened to you that day?' she asked. I wished I could explain it to her but she wouldn't understand.

'I blanked out and forgot everything,' I mumbled. She nodded in an understanding manner. I walked back to my desk holding my paper in my hand. Oddly enough, I wasn't upset that I had failed Chemistry. It would be tough explaining it to my parents but I would manage.

I looked at my paper again and winced when I read

some of the answers I had copied from Chaya. In at least two answers, the word 'birthday' had crept up.

'Hydrogen is combustible but doesn't support birthdays.'

'Combines with chlorine to form hydrogen chloride birthday.'

I shook my head, wondering if I could plug my ears with cotton before the next exam.

Behind me, Lekha had started singing softly 'Oonchi hai building, lift teri band hai' softly. Noooo!

Welcome Home, Sugar

HARSHIKAA UDASI

Today he was going to do it. With the right balance
of logic and emotional appeal, it shouldn't be difficult,
he thought. He had spent the night chalking out the
strategy and working out exactly what he would say.
'You won't win against her. Moms are the best,' a
sharp voice said to him. Varun scowled at where the
voice came from and marched out of his room. Oh
why were his thoughts so transparent?

'Ma, do you have that guy's number?' he asked his
mom who was busy watering her plants. She looked up
quizzically. But before she could react, he continued,
'No, no. Pa has it, now I remember.'

'Which guy, Varun?' she asked.

'Nothing, Ma. It's okay,' he said, disappearing into
his room. That should have just aroused her interest,
he smiled to himself.

Varun-1. Ma-0.

'She'll still win. Moms have sensors,' the voice said
again. The boy just ignored it now.

Ten minutes later, his mom hollered to him, 'Varun, come for breakfast, will you?' He dragged himself out of his room, Biology book in hand. Slamming the book down on the table, he began to butter his toast. 'Didn't Pa say he is going to be in a day-long meeting today?' he asked, turning towards her, muttering, 'I am so dead.'

'How many times have I told you I want good language when you are with your family?' Ma said. 'And "so dead" is not even correct English.' Trust her to check his grammar even when he is telling her he is dying, or is dead, or in some phase of basically getting there.

Ma-1. Varun-1.

He could almost hear the voice in his room laughing at him now. 'Sorry,' he mumbled. Ma seemed to be losing focus and it was time to bring her back on track. 'Do you think Pa will take my calls during lunchtime at least?' he ventured again.

'I don't know! Why can't you just tell me why you are trying to contact him?' she said, looking exasperated.

Bingo, this was the right time!

'I want that that guy's number—the one who fixed the Jinsoku charger last month. It seems to have conked off again. She runs out of power every other hour and I just can't study for my exams,' he shrugged. 'Today, the battery won't last for more than ten minutes!' Just the right pitch of voice, the right words, the right expression. Not a notch higher, nor lower. The reaction was just as he had thought it would be. 'So soon? We paid him a bomb for repairing it. Get the charger here. Let me have a look,' she said in alarm.

Varun-2. Ma-1.

Now he needed to play it cool to clear this stage and move on to the next. He sauntered into his room, removed the charger before the voice could say anything and lugged it out.

At 5 kilograms, this was one heavy charger for an AI robot. Then again, Jinsoku belonged to the first generation of AI robots. The company brochure had said they were innovating constantly and in the next couple of years a sleeker robot with a lighter and longer-lasting battery would be out.

When Jinsoku aka Jinny came home last year to assist Varun in his exams, he was thrilled. As the first of her tribe, she was not particularly blessed in the looks department but she excelled in Maths, Science and History, and was above average in English Comprehension. However, she still needed help with composing English essays. Varun's parents, especially Pa, were a little sceptical of shelling out an obscenely high amount for a 'creature' that they didn't particularly like, but then almost all the kids in Varun's school had bought one nearly six months ago.

With Jinny there to help him, his parents no longer needed to send him to coaching classes. Who went to a drab coaching class when there was a smarter option available? The kids no longer needed to commute, nor sit with a hundred other kids in a cramped room, besides, of course, not spending another fortune on eating out and hanging out with their coaching class friends. If you were somebody who had any sense (and a fair bit of money, too) Jinsoku was your option. She came at a price that was 25 per cent higher than the coaching class fee. But with a life expectancy of two years, she seemed a better investment, his parents had thought. Pa had required some nudging by Ma, though.

When Jinny arrived, she freaked them out. To begin with, they hated the idea of a girl sharing room space with their son. 'Mom, I am eleven, and she is an AI robot for heavens' sake!' Varun had protested. But they were suspicious. Especially Pa. 'Can't understand the need for AI robots,' he grumbled. 'We studied for our exams and wrote our exams. Your cousin Shivani is just five years older and she did that too. This AI culture is just all wrong.' But Ma countered his argument with, 'Cut him some slack, Shubho! That's so last generation!' Attagirl, Mom! However, Ma disliked how human Jinny looked. It was almost like someone was watching over you all the time and she found it creepy.

The product description said Jinny was twenty years old. The makers had given her as many human qualities as they could. So Varun knew that Jinsoku meant 'swift' in Japanese, that she liked playing tennis and that she loved roses over jasmine. Which means, obviously, that she was programmed for it all.

Though Varun was among the last few in his class to get an AI robot, she also had a couple of additional features over the existing ones. Her grip over the pen was twice better than her predecessors, and she could speak Sinhalese and Bhutanese too. Varun didn't know where he would use that but it was an additional feature alright!

With Jinny, preparing for exams was a thrilling adventure. The kids would have loved it even more if all they had to do was scan the texts in the Jinsoku scanner. But schools had sent strict instructions to the parents to password-protect that feature. They seemed serious about it because there were thorough checks every morning before class. Children had to make some effort after all! So reading to Jinny was compulsory.

Varun didn't mind that. All he had to do was charge Jinny up and read the entire lesson to her. He had to stop only if she couldn't understand his accent. But that was a problem that everybody had already faced with Siri, Google Assistant, and Alexa. The real difference here was that Jinny was Japanese. But Varun had a handy solution for that—an app that let him speak English with a Japanese accent.

Once Jinny was fed the information, she was good to go. She could read the questions and pull out the right answer with her search engine program—and not just multiple choice ones but also long-answer format! She could not understand a thing, but she was a pro at being 'statistically correct'. For History and Geography comprehension questions, she could put her keyword mining skills to use and pull out the right answers every time.

Her real test, and a dicey one too, was the 250-

word essay on any topic, a compulsory question in the English paper. Varun still remembered the first exam, where Jinny was asked to write about 'Your experience at the summer boot camp'.

This was all she had managed:

I was part of a short-lived rap duo L'il Soldiers that had a single album named Boot Camp in 1999. For this I went to a school in North America called Combat School, undergoing basic training at a United States Marine Corps Recruit Training camp, also known as a boot camp. It had students from varied backgrounds, from those who had master's degrees in computer science to a Starbucks barista. Boot camps are criticized around the world for their lack of behavioural change and for the way extreme force can traumatize children and youngsters.

Well, essays were not really her forte. But Varun aced the rest of the exams. 98.9 per cent overall! Along with eighteen others of his class, Jinsoku owners all.

But now, over a year later, Varun was getting seriously creeped out by Jinny. With her artificial intelligence, she was able to read Varun's thoughts, especially when he thought of really nasty or naughty things to do. Besides being super creepy, it was getting super annoying.

When she did it two months ago for the first time, Varun was completely dumbstruck. He had complained of a tummy ache to his mother but Jinny had ratted on him. 'He wants to avoid the *baingan* dish you have cooked,' she informed Ma. Why eat something that's called eggplant but is not anywhere close to being an egg, was Varun's defence, as Ma glared at him. Then there was the time when Jinny had accompanied him to school. When he told his classmate Ragini, the nosy one, that he didn't have the notes she was asking for, Jinny had interrupted their conversation to 'gently' remind him that they were in the third compartment of his schoolbag. 'Right within the pages of your Science 2 notebook,' she added, helpfully.

Varun had to do something about her. What was the oldest trick in the book to ensure that a chargeable device stops functioning? Overcharging, of course! He knew that about mobile phones. He would work that one here too!

Varun's thoughts were interrupted by a loud snap. Ma had opened up the Jinsoku battery completely, and it didn't look too good. Varun knew an amazing thing about his parents—they were both hopeless around gadgets. Pa was an architect and Ma a drummer. While they aced their jobs, when it came to reassembling broken-down gadgets, they drew a blank. To her credit, Ma at least tried. Pa didn't even venture there.

Presently, she stood over the dismembered parts of Jinny wondering how to save the situation.

'Err, Varun, I think we will have to check with that battery guy again. Meanwhile, which part goes next?' she asked, sheepishly. 'I don't know Ma, I thought you were in control here,' Varun said, adding, 'Doesn't this look sort of, broken beyond repair? This bit is looking puffed up, it won't fit back.'

'I'll figure it out. You go and study for now. You have just a month left for your finals, and isn't today your Biology day?' she asked. Varun put on a helpless act. 'But Ma, how can I study without Jinny?'

'What is that supposed to mean, young man?' she replied sharply.

'You know...it's difficult...I am so used to her...it's near impossible actually,' he murmured.

'Oh. Is it?' she said with a steely look in her eyes.

Varun slunk away but not before strategically placing a new product brochure at his mom's workstation.

In the evening, when his father returned home, the situation was still bleak. 'Pa, I have been without Jinny today. ALL day!' Varun complained, looking at his mother from the corner of his eye.

'And that is supposed to be a problem? I am so happy she's conked off!' was his curt response.

Varun couldn't believe his father was actually delighted. While Pa did not like Varun's dependence on Jinny, her arrival also meant he had not been bothered for chemical equations that he had forgotten two decades ago and for historical characters whose names he didn't know how to spell, least of all remember the wars they fought.

'Pa, please call the guy who repaired her battery last time, will you?' Varun pleaded. 'I am not able to study the way I used to before Jinny came in. She's made it much simpler and organized.'

'I think AI robots answering exams should be declared illegal. Isn't there a law in our country against this?' Varun's dad asked no one in particular. But Ma was always there to answer any redundant questions.

'Shubho, I think you need to be transported to the twentieth century. Jinny was super helpful, okay?'

Was? Had Varun heard the word 'was'?

'What do you mean "was"? Let's get her battery repaired and give it back to this lazy kid,' Pa replied.

'Uh, well. The battery can't be repaired. I may have sort of, a little, I mean... accidently spoilt it,' Ma replied.

'You WHAT? You jolly well know there isn't a battery replacement!'

Well, that was how the big fight began. Varun returned to his room. He tried studying a little Biology. He ventured out for a sandwich. The fight was still on, having now reached the issue of leaking taps and faulty dryers in the house, with Ma winning it. He went back to his room and turned on the headphones to cut the noise out, and nodded off to sleep. When he woke up the two had mellowed down and were instead fighting about their choice of vegetables. Varun looked at his watch. He would give it five more minutes.

In exactly five minutes his parents came into his room.

Match point.

'How's it going, champ?' Pa asked. Varun nodded, pretending to look busy studying the insides of amphibians. 'We have some news for you. Keeping in mind your amazing performance all through last year, along with Jinny of course, and considering that she isn't working to her potential, we have decided to buy you the latest AI robot model in the market—the Sugureta 7.1,' said Ma.

'We can go tomorrow to the store and pick her up. Hey! Don't look like you are missing Jinny. Change is the name of the game, champ. And what luck that we got the product brochure delivered today!' said Pa, nodding at Mom.

Concealing his excitement, Varun nodded and bid them good night.

When his parents left, he turned to his phone and checked out the technical specs of Sugureta as he had several times earlier: *The Sugureta 7.1 (Japanese for excellent) comes with face recognition, voice recognition and touch recognition. She comes with a superior grip, a fast-loading memory and a battery lasting upto 120 hours. Her outstanding features include multipoint cameras with embedded sensors that allow her to express herself using body language along with verbal communication. Sugureta has been trained specifically to answer exams and has a memory base corresponding to the cloud network. She has been trained to answer long-format questions concisely and with precision, and can offer opinions. Presenting Sugureta, the most human AI robot from the Mirai Corp.*

'Game over,' he said, looking at Jinny. Sugar was coming home. It was a good thing he had left that brochure about the latest AI robots within Ma's reach, wasn't it?

Expected Results

PAYAL DHAR

Misha loved to hang out at Bishan Kaka's chaotic cycle shop. It was called Super Cycle Repairs and Sales, and it was the most exciting place ever. There was a delicious array of polished shiny bicycles, from the little kids' ones with their jaunty baskets and bright colours, to the grown-up ones with great thick tyres and solid frames. The bicycles spilled out on to the footpath, lined up along the front of the stop, and little tricycles in gaudy colours hung from the awning above them. Usually, there was a mechanic out in the front, either mending a puncture or assembling a cycle. It was fascinating to watch the bits and pieces coming together to form an actual, working bicycle.

'Come to admire my cycles again?' Bishan Kaka's booming voice called out. 'Are you going to buy one today?'

Misha smiled at the elderly man. He asked her that almost every day. 'I might. I like this red one.' Indeed, it was beautiful, chrome red with silver highlights. It seemed a bit big for her, but she was sure she'd grow into it. She ran her hands over the shiny handlebars with their black and red grips, and asked the question she'd been avoiding for months: 'How much is this, Bishan Kaka?'

He regarded her over his spectacles. He seemed to think long and hard, so much so that Misha thought he wouldn't reply at all.

'It's around three thousand rupees.'

Misha's heart sank. That was more than money than she'd ever had.

But Bishan Kaka went on. 'But I will give you a very good discount.' Then he finally smiled again.

Misha wanted to ask how much discount, and whether it would cost her anywhere close to the seven hundred rupees that she had had saved up—that itself had taken her years to cobble together. But she didn't. She smiled back. She had a weird sort of pain deep inside her stomach. She didn't have a word for that feeling, but she knew it was there because she wanted a cycle so badly.

With a sigh, she dragged herself away, her shoulders slumped, as she traipsed home. That hollow feeling clawed away inside her.

Nasir Kaka was coming down the lane from the other end as Misha reached home. He had a briefcase in one hand and a bag of groceries in the other.

'Hello,' he said as he came closer. 'Had a good day?'

Misha shrugged as she held the gate open for him.

'It was okay. Nasir Kaka, how long do you think it'll take for me to earn three thousand rupees?'

'Why do you need so much money?'

She told him about the cycle. 'I'm going to save and save and save till I have enough to buy it.'

'Good for you. That's exactly how I bought my first cycle, too.'

This is what Misha liked about Nasir Kaka—he could be counted upon to be supportive. Ma or Baba would have just said that she was too young to earn any money or something like that. He wasn't her real uncle, though. He was her father's oldest friend—they used to be in school together eons ago. Recently, he had moved into the barsaati on the terrace of their house.

'How can I earn some money?' she asked him as they rang the bell. 'Do you think I'm too young to get a job?'

He frowned. 'Probably. But there could be other ways.'

Misha perked up. 'Like?'

'Well, maybe you could make something to sell.'

'I'm good at drawing. Maybe I can sell some drawings.'

Before Nasir Kala could respond, the door opened and Ma was standing there, her face like thunder. She waved a sheet of paper, and with a sinking heart Misha recognized her Bangla unit test paper that she had been hiding in her bag for two days.

***

'Look at this, just look. Full of red marks!'

Misha bent her head so her chin touched her chest. She didn't really care that she had got three out of twenty-five, but she knew from experience that she had to pretend it was a big deal.

'Don't you realize how bad this looks? Your father is the principal of the school and his only daughter is going to repeat class six. What are people going to say?'

It wasn't the sort of question that she would have expected an answer for, so Misha remained silent, wincing as her mother smacked the test paper down on the table.

'That's it then. No TV, no computer, no friends, no going out till your final exams are over. You are going to spend all your time studying.'

'But Ma...' began Misha in dismay.

'Don't "but Ma" me. You should have thought of it before. How come you get twenty-five on twenty-five in Maths but can't manage to write one correct sentence in your own mother tongue, hain? Tell me that. Running around in the market all day. You are almost twelve years old, you have to learn to be responsible.'

Her mother stormed out the room, and Nasir Kaka, pottering about in the dining room just outside and pretending not to hear anything, turned towards her as she passed. 'Boudi, can I have a word?'

Misha watched Ma and Nasir Kaka conferring in low voice. Ma turned and glanced at Misha, then looked away. Misha got up and ran outside into the balcony, hot tears threatening to spill. There was still more than a month for the final exams. How would she survive without TV and not going out? Those cycles were not going to admire themselves.

A few minutes later, Nasir Kaka came and stood next to her. 'So.' He crossed his arms and looked down at Misha. 'Do you want the good news or the bad news?'

Misha shrugged. 'There's nothing good in my life any more.' She turned away, leaning on the balcony railing and staring out at their tiny, overgrown garden, the lemon tree just inches from her face.

'Good or bad?' Nasir Kaka persisted.

'Might as well tell me the bad news first.'

'All right, then. Starting from Monday, every evening, when I come back from office, I'm going to help you with your school work. For two hours every day. We will first do whatever homework you have, then we'll revise the course for your final exams.'

'Fine.' That wasn't as bad as she'd expected. It wasn't just that she hated lessons, it was that she couldn't get her head around most things, at least not the way the teachers taught at her school. Maths was the only thing that made sense. Maybe it was a good thing if Nasir Kaka explained a few things to her.

Then a thought struck her. If the bad wasn't so bad, what was the good thing? She turned to Nasir Kaka. 'What's the good news?'

'Your Ma has agreed that there's no need to punish you if you promise to work with me.'

Misha's face broke into a grin. 'Really?'

'Yes, really. And,' Nasir Kaka leaned down next to her, 'if you keep up your end of the bargain and study hard, I will help you buy your bicycle.'

'*Really?*'

'Absolutely.'

But Misha's elation faded by the time she was getting into bed that night. The bargain wasn't going to be as simple to keep as she had thought.

***

'But this is fantastic!' Anya exclaimed. 'You got out of a punishment, and if you study with your Kaka every day, you will get your cycle too? I think that's called a win-win situation.'

'You're missing the most important thing. You know as well as I do that the chances of my acing the exams are a big fat zero. Just like the one I got in my History test, when I had to fake Ma's signature.'

The girls fell silent, though Misha's brain was working feverishly. She wanted that cycle so badly. She *had* to find a way to crack the exams. She turned to her best friend. 'What do you know about making chits?'

Anya's eyes went round. 'You mean like,' her voice dropped to a whisper, 'chits for exams?'

'Mmhmm.'

'You're going to *cheat?*'

'I have to, don't I?'

Anya blinked in confusion. Obviously, cheating in

exams had never occurred to Anya—her test papers were filled with tick marks and 'very goods'.

'I saw a movie once where a boy had written everything in very small letters on his arm,' Misha went on, undeterred. 'But I can't write the entire course on my arms. It won't fit. Anyway, everyone will see it. It has to be chits, Anya. But I don't know how to hide them.'

Anya didn't say anything. She looked uncomfortable. Misha felt a stab of annoyance towards her. She was such a goody two-shoes.

On her way home that afternoon, Misha dawdled in the market, popping in at Bishan Kaka's again. 'So, are you buying the cycle today?' he twinkled at her.

Misha laughed, but it set her thinking. *Maybe I'm looking at it wrong. I should focus on how to get money for the cycle. That's the important thing.*

***

'Are you mad?' Pranoy snatched his Maths homework notebook away. 'Two *hundred* rupees?'

'Okay, okay!' Misha pulled at the notebook. 'Give me hundred.'

'I'll give you twenty-five.'

'You're in class Seven and I'm only in class Six but I can still do your homework. So I want fifty.'

'Fine!'

Misha clenched her teeth and went to her seat with Pranoy's homework. Anya was sitting on Misha's desk, looking at her with narrowed eyes.

'What are you doing?'

'Earning some money.'

'What? Why?'

'For the cycle, silly. I'm never going to get great marks in the exams, am I? So I have decided to stop worrying about them and start earning some money.'

'By doing Pranoy's homework?'

'Not just his. I'm offering a service. Maths homework for two hundred bucks.'

'You're mad.' Anya shook her head and went back to eating her tiffin.

Two girls from class 6B looked inside their classroom, both clutching notebooks to their chests.

'Are you Misha?' one of them called.

'Yeah.'

'Pranoy said you're doing Maths homework for fifty bucks.'

'Two hundred.'

'Whoa.' The other girl rolled her eyes and pulled at her friend's sleeve.

'Wait,' Misha called. 'I have early-bird discounts.'

That afternoon, Misha walked home with a heavy heart and forty-seven rupees in her pocket. Rukmini had had only twenty bucks, and Pranoy had had twenty-five, and Alia just some coins. They'd all promised to bring the rest of the money on Monday, but somehow Misha had an idea that this line of business was not going to work out. She would have to work out a new plan for next week.

***

On Monday, at break time, Misha arranged her drawing things on her desk. She pulled out a piece of card that she had carefully prepared over the weekend and set it against her pencil-box. It said: 'Art for sale. Cards, scenery & portraits. Readymade & on order.' In smaller text underneath was written, 'Payment in advance.'

A couple of her classmates sauntered by. 'What are you doing?' Shammi smirked.

Misha glared at her. 'I'm selling my art, can't you read?'

Arushi picked up a card on which there was a watercolour of three dancing cats. 'What is this? Happy Cat Day?'

Misha snatched it back. 'It's a blank card. You can use it for anything. Do you want to buy it? Fifty bucks.'

'Who'll pay fifty for *this*?'

'It's a unique piece,' said Misha with as much superiority as she could muster.

'You!' cried a voice. Pranoy burst into the room, his face red. 'I'm in trouble because of you. Give me my money back!'

Misha stood up, hands on her hips. 'You give me the rest of my money!'

'My Maths teacher called my parents because you did my homework!'

'What? That doesn't even make sense.'

Arushi and Shammi watched the altercation with interest. A few others gathered around, sensing a fight.

'The answers were all correct, and Miss said I cheated from the Internet,' said poor Pranoy.

'Of course the answers were all correct,' Misha replied. 'If you wanted to get them all wrong you could have done it all yourself. Now, where's my money?'

'You give me *my* money back.'

'Make me.'

'Children!' The voice of Misha's class teacher was like a bucket of cold water. The crowd melted away as she came into the room and frowned at the arrangement on Misha's desk. 'What is this?'

'I, um,' she quickly swept the card advertising her wares off the table, 'was making some drawings.'

Her teacher's eyes narrowed. 'Really? Well, you'd better wrap up. Don't let me catch you selling things in school ever again.'

Misha's face burned as she put away her things, especially because she could see Shammi and Arushi still sniggering from the corner. She felt dejected. Her business ventures had all gone bust even before they could take off properly.

'Miss said "Don't let me *catch* you selling things,"' she said to Anya later, 'which means I have to find a way to sell something so she doesn't catch me.'

'If you put your brain to studying instead of coming up with harebrained schemes, you might actually be able to solve your problems.'

Misha glared at her. Sometimes Anya just didn't understand what was important.

***

'What happened? You seem distracted today,' Nasir Kaka said in the middle of Geography that evening.

Misha put her pen down. 'Did you think of any other ways in which I could earn money?' she asked him.

Nasir Kaka shook his head. 'I didn't, I'm sorry.' He frowned. 'But why do you need to earn money?'

'For the cycle, of course. You forgot?'

'No, no, I didn't forget. It's just that we've been doing so well these past few days with your lessons. I did promise to buy you your cycle if you studied hard, remember?'

'Yes, I know, Nasir Kaka, but,' she turned her head and looked straight into his eyes, 'you know I'm never going to get through with flying colours, no matter how hard I try. Right?'

Nasir Kaka's eyes narrowed. 'With that attitude, you're not going to get anywhere.'

'But you know what I mean?' Misha persisted.

'All I know is that you should focus on the matter at hand. There are less than three weeks left for your exams.'

Misha sighed and went back to filling states and union territories on a political map of India. The trouble with grown-ups was that their priorities were all messed up.

To Misha's alarm, the days rolled by faster than she could come up with a new business idea. School was hectic enough, and at home Nasir Kaka kept her nose to the grindstone. Thankfully, he was patient and didn't get angry when Misha didn't understand things or got them wrong. He just found different ways to explain them, and kept at it till they made sense to her. One day, Misha shocked herself by writing a whole one-page essay in Bangla on her favourite book, with just nine spelling mistakes.

Even her jaunts to the market were curtailed these days as Ma wanted her home, revising. The teachers were also keeping an extra eye on them, so it wasn't like Misha could try another scheme easily. In fact, she was so busy that she actually forgot to worry, and it was only the weekend before the exams were due to start that she remembered with a start her original idea of needing to prepare chits.

She lingered outside her father's study, where the computer was, and wondered if she could get a chance to slip inside and do a quick Google search. But then, Baba only let her use the Internet when he was around, and there was no way she could risk it.

A pall of gloom descended around Misha on the last evening before her first exam, which, fortunately, was Maths, the only subject she was confident about. Nasir Kaka mistook her low spirits as exam nerves and tried his best to cheer her up. Ma made Misha's favourite *payesh* (without raisins). But it was still with a heavy heart that Misha went to bed.

***

Exam week went by in a blur till Misha woke up on Saturday morning with an incredible feeling of lightness. There were no more exams!

She gobbled down her breakfast and raced to the market as soon as she could.

'Do you have any jobs in your shop?' she asked Bishan Kaka.

'What?'

'I need to earn the money to buy that cycle,' Misha explained to him. 'I only have seven hundred and forty-seven rupees right now. I can learn to fix bicycles. I'm very good at stuff like that.'

Bishan Kaka laughed. 'Oh, Misha. I couldn't employ you. It would be against the law, for one thing. For another, I don't need any more help than I have.'

'Oh.' Misha's heart plummeted.

'Look, I can sell you the cycle on instalment. How about I talk to your Baba about it?'

'No,' said Misha, her face turned towards the floor so he couldn't see the tears pooling in her eyes. 'I don't think I did well in my exams, you see. He's not going to buy me a cycle now.'

'I'm sorry, Misha,' said Bishan Kaka sympathetically.

'It's okay. It's not your fault.'

The results came out ten days later, and as Misha had predicted, hers were well below average. Except for Maths—there she had come out with flying colours. The good thing was that she hadn't failed anything. In fact, she had managed a pretty decent score in History and Science.

'It's not so bad,' Anya tried to buoy her sagging mood. 'You only lost two marks in maths. That's better than me.'

'Yeah, but you are first in class,' Misha pointed out. 'I am third from bottom.'

There was nothing Anya could say to that. They watched Misha's mother talking to their class teacher, both of them looking very serious.

'What do you think they're saying?' Anya asked.

'Plotting to lock me in a room forever,' Misha replied gloomily. Ma finished her conversation and then moved away to make a call on her mobile. *Probably calling Baba to tell him what a failure I am, though he already knows.*

Misha and her mother left the school in silence and hailed an auto-rickshaw because Ma didn't like walking all that much.

'Are you mad at me?' Misha asked when the silence started to feel oppressive.

'No, no,' Ma replied.

Misha gave her an incredulous look. 'Oh come on. Look at my results. I know you're going to give me a lecture about how disappointed you are.'

'Misha...' Ma sighed. 'I'm not. I was thinking about what your teacher said. See, you're brilliant at Maths, but not in other subjects. She thinks...well, there are a couple of other children like you in the school. From next month, a special teacher is going to come to take some extra classes with you.'

'What, more classes?' Misha wailed. 'So this is my punishment?'

'It's not a punishment. She thinks you need to be taught in a different way. We'll see if that works.'

Misha looked at her mother through the corner of her eyes. It didn't matter how she put it, it still sounded dire. They reached home in silence, and Misha was surprised when Nasir Kaka opened the door.

'You didn't go to office?' she asked.

'I took some time off. So you got your result?'

She handed him the report card, standing before him, arms crossed, as he studied it. When he finally finished, he shut it and put in the table.

'I'm sorry,' Misha said in a low voice.

'Why?'

'Because you worked so hard and...'

'No. You worked so hard.' Nasir Kaka tapped her shoulder. 'Follow me.'

He led her through the house, Ma following, out to the little garden at the back. And there, on the balcony, stood a shiny red and silver bicycle.

Misha gasped. She felt light-headed and had to reach for the doorframe to support herself. 'What...' she managed to croak, 'is that?'

'We had a deal,' Nasir Kaka replied.

'But...I didn't do well.'

'That wasn't the deal. It was to study hard, try your best. You did that.'

'I...' Misha looked at Nasir Kaka and then at Ma, who smiled. 'It's really mine?'

It really was.

A Zgnogir in Mumbai

SHABNAM MINWALLA

It was no fun being a zgnogir. That was what Zgn8713 decided as he plodded through the inky night, clutching a raggedy bundle of paper.

An angry wind whipped through the trees, scattering leaves and shrieking past houses. It was the perfect night for scaring small children in striped pajamas and nervous old ladies clutching handbags. All the Undead would be out and about, showing their fangs and spreading terror.

Except the zgnogir. They would be busy writing yet another exam.

'Afterlife is so unfair,' Zgn8713 whined to himself, kicking a stone with decaying feet. 'We are as undead as vampires. We smell as disgusting as ghouls. We can roll our eyeballs just as creepily as zombies. So why isn't anybody afraid of us?'

Zgn8713 was a bit of a whiner. But this time he was not exaggerating. It was an unfortunate fact that nobody was afraid of the zgnogir. Nobody made movies called *Zgnogir Diaries* or *Night of the Zgnogir* or *Pride and Prejudice and Zgnogir*. Not even Wikipedia spared a single line for them.

This neglect stemmed from a tricky problem. Nobody had heard of the zgnogir.

New vampires were put through a weekend workshop on bloodsucking and allowed to go about their thirsty business. Young zombies were shown a few YouTube videos and let loose to feed on brains and shed a few smelly body parts. Inexperienced ghouls were given a book on basic shapeshifting (from fork to spider to Justin Bieber—then back to fork) and sent out to do their thing.

But did the zgnogir take this easy way out? Oh no.

All zgnogir had to pass twenty-nine exams before they were considered ready to venture into the human world.

They had to know the calorie content of the cerebrum, the hamstring muscles and of toes.

They had to draw diagrams of the adrenal gland and label all the bits and bobs.

They had to know the words for 'Fear of Cockroaches' and 'Fear of Ghosts'. And they had to spell them correctly.

They had to write essay-type answers on 'How to Scare a Waiter in a Dark Restaurant' and 'Why Wolves Howl at the Moon'.

Very few zgnogir passed all twenty-nine exams. Those who managed were so exhausted after all their tuition classes and sleepless days that they were as spine-chilling as a crumpled tablecloth. Literally.

On a good night, the zgnogir were bloodcurdlingly ghastly. They were dead white creatures with glaring red eyes and snaky movement. Hissy, gurgly sounds emerged from grey lips.

On a bad night, though, when they were low on energy, they tended to deflate into something that looked like an unwashed bedsheet. And human beings could be merciless with unwashed bedsheets, as Zgn3003 had found some weeks ago.

Zgn3003 was last year's exam topper and the Hope of the Zgnogir. He was the hero who would introduce the world to a scourge more lethal than dengue, than Dracula, than even Donald Trump. He would teach wimpy vampires and meddlesome mummies a thing or two. He would make sure that 'zgnogir' was the Number One trending search on Google.

The Hope of the Zgnogir set out amidst speeches and bone-banging. He slunk back home a week later, looking like a limp sock. Even worse, a limp sock smelling of Surf Excelmatic.

The details emerged a few nights later.

'He fell asleep while he was haunting an apartment in Bangalore,' Zgn5552 whispered during a deathday party in the graveyard. 'He woke up in a washing machine filled with wet towels and bathmats. It was horrid.'

'He hardly comes out of his tomb any more,' Zgn8713 agreed. 'And he still smells of soap. It's so disappointing. I really thought he would make us famous.'

At this moment, though, Zgn8713 had bigger worries. Like the exam on Ancient and Medieval History. Zgn8713 was bad with dates and ancient dynasties. He knew he was going to fail this exam. Which meant that his parents wouldn't get him the ZgniPhone that that he wanted so desperately.

'Which Undead Warrior was created when a pregnant black cat leapt over a coffin during the Qing dynasty in China? Oh, oh...' Zgn8713 riffled through the brittle notes in his hand, feeling frantic.

Outside the examination crypt, he spotted his friends. Zgn5552 was giving a brilliant lecture on the Undead and the Crusades. Everybody else was nodding knowledgably. 'Why, oh why do I have to be such a duffer?' Zgn8713 moped, as he slunk into the crypt and arranged his pens and erasers.

Five minutes later, the head examiner slithered into the room. Usually, she got right down to business, handing out exam papers and gloating. Today, though, she was accompanied by two official-looking zgnogir. Both were hideously skeletal and stinky, and obviously very senior in the Zgnogir Administration.

The reeksome threesome stood at the door and glared till the room became as silent as a tomb (though tombs occupied by vampires, zombies and zgnogir can be pretty noisy at times). Then Almost Skeleton One hissed through grey lips, 'Good midnight. We are here to talk to you about an important problem. We are very concerned about our poor image in the human world. So we have appointed a consultant to look into the matter. He believes that our education system is too dependent on books and rote learning. He has recommended field trips and projects.'

'We zgnogir, as you know, believe in doing things perfectly,' Almost Skeleton Two interrupted. 'We believe in being perfectly prepared before going into the human world. But apparently we need to change with the times. So you have a choice today. You can appear for your exam, or you can choose to go on a Mini Mission.'

The room exploded with gasps and grunts and the Head Examiner gave a ghastly laugh. 'There is no pressure to go on this reckless mission. I hope you understand that?'

The students nodded. The Head Examiner smirked at the Almost Skeletons. 'Everyone would rather do the exam,' she said. 'Please communicate that to His Decomposeship. I don't think this foolish idea will work.'

That was when Zgn8713 found his voice. 'Sirs, Ma'am,' he mumbled. 'What do we have to do on the Mini Mission?'

'Go among the humans and frighten at least one of them,' Almost Skeleton One chuckled. 'Quite ridiculous, yes?'

Everybody chuckled along. Everybody, except Zgn8713.

'If I do the Mini Mission, will I have to appear for the Medieval History exam?' he asked instead.

'No,' Almost Skeleton Two replied. 'But it's much easier to pass the exam. Not even the brilliant Zgn3003...'

Zgn8713 thought fast. He had no chance of passing the exam. He had a minuscule chance of succeeding in the mission. Minuscule was better than zero. So he raised his hand and croaked, 'I will do the Mini Mission.' The class muttered. The officials frowned. Zgn8713 was lead out of the crypt and given instructions. Tomorrow night he would follow an underground path to a human city. There, he had to frighten one human being and return with proof.

Zgn8713 was given a copy of *Techniques of Terror: Strategies to Frighten Humans Half to Death*. The book was based on intensive research and Zgn8713 read it twice. The book had chapters with headings like 'How to choose your victims' and 'How to introduce yourself to your victims'.

At 9 p.m., a sullen zgnogir led Zgn8713 through tunnels and sewers to an open manhole. He spoke twice. The first time to complain about his hip pain. The second time to point at the manhole and grunt, 'Up is Mumbai.'

Bewildered, Zgn8713 climbed out of the manhole. He looked around, gawping at the streetlights that tinged the night with orange and the buildings that loomed before him. For the first time he wished he had just appeared for the stupid exam instead.

Well, too late now.

Zgn8713 wandered the silent streets and took a few quick pictures for Zgn5552. Then he huddled in a corner, reread the first chapter of *Techniques of Terror* and practiced a few nasty faces. Finally, he glided to a building and slithered up and down, peering into all the windows.

Three buildings later, he found exactly what he was looking for—an open window leading into the bedroom of a little girl. 'Aha,' he thought to himself, glugging with satisfaction. '*Technique of Terror* says that this is the perfect victim.'

Zgn8713 crawled into the pink bedroom. He was just wondering whether to pounce or howl when the little girl under the blanket opened her eyes. She looked confused for a moment, and then delighted.

'What is my present?' she asked in a bright, singsong voice.

'Huh?' Zgn8713 said. *Technique of Terror* hadn't mentioned presents.

'My present?' the girl repeated. 'Last time you gave me glittery stickers. What are you giving me this time?'

'No present,' Zgn8713 said indignantly. Zgnogir spread fear and misery, not glittery stickers. This was not going according to plan.

'Aren't you the tooth fairy?' the little girl snapped. 'You have to give me a present. Have to, have to, have to.'

Zgn8713 shuddered. There could be no greater insult to the zgnogir than being confused with a fairy. He cleared his throat, made a cross-eyed face, and emitted a chilling laugh. 'I am...I am...' he groaned, trying to think of the names that *Techniques of Terror* had recommended. 'I am...I AM...MONACO.'

'But Monaco is a biscuit,' the girl protested, looking more hungry than scared. 'Do you have biscuit?'

'Not Monaco, Mogambo,' Zgn8713 corrected himself quickly. 'My name is MOGAMBO and I am...I am...I am going to eat you up.'

'But you don't have any teeth,' the child replied. 'I know who you are. You are a BAD Tooth Fairy and you are trying to steal my tooth because your teeth have fallen out. But you can't have my tooth unless you give me a PRESENT.'

Zgn8713 was getting alarmed. He wished he could read a few pages of *Techniques of Terror*. Instead, he tried to remember the section on 'Wicked Threats'. 'Keep quiet,' he hissed. 'If you don't keep quiet I will...I will...I will tie you upside down from a rope dangling above a pool full of piranhas and crocodiles. Then when the rope breaks you will fall into the lake and they will eat you up.'

The little girl was silent for a minute. Then she wailed, 'You are hurting my feelings.'

Zgn8713 was stumped—but he tried once more. He opened his mouth and emitted a green vomit, even sludgier than the ones in *Techniques of Terror*. The little girl should have been shivering. Instead she glared and started throwing cushions and teddy bears at poor Zgn8713. 'That rug was from my aunty in London. Go away, you bad Tooth Fairy. You spoiled my fluffy wuffy.'

Whimpering, Zgn8713 headed for the window. A child who was unbothered by splodgy green vomit was a scary creature. A child who called a rug a fluffy wuffy was even worse. He was afraid for his afterlife.

Zgn8713 was almost out of the window when the bedroom door opened and a sleepy man poked his head into the room. 'What happened, Trisha baby?' he said. 'Why are you...'

At that moment the man caught sight of Zgn8713— rotting limbs, red eyes, green vomit and all. He let out a long moan, sank to his knees and fell onto the vomit-covered rug in a faint.

Zgn8713 did not waste a moment. He whipped out his phone to capture this historic moment. Just then a woman rushed into the room. 'Can you all stop making such a—aaaaahh, aaaaah! Help! Heeeeeelppppp! Ayeee—eee—eeeeee!'

Zgn8713 shot a video of the unconscious man and the hysterical woman. Then he cast one last glare upon Trisha and climbed out of the window, down the drainpipe and into the manhole. He reached home a few hours later to a hero's welcome.

His Decomposeship himself gave Zgn8713 the latest model ZgniPhone. His parents bought him a cool phone case that looked like it was made from intestines.

Zgn8713 has never had to attempt another exam. He now organizes regular field trips up the manhole to Mumbai. He and his students have scared quite a few people on their way home from parties and work. They have printed a set of business cards stating, 'You have just met a ZGNOGIR. Fear for your life.'

Wikipedia will soon be featuring a page on the Dreaded Zgnogir—and Zgn8713 can't wait.

Books Alive

JANE DE SUZA

'Who says helium is He. It may be She!'

On the night before the exams began, Akanksha slammed her book shut. 'I hate Chemistry!'

'And I hate History! I hate exams!' Himanshu, her brother, followed her, stomping out of the study sleepily, shutting the door behind them with a bang. The exams loomed large and scary.

Something else laid in wait too. Though they'd never have believed it.

Hardly had the last light faded and the gentle snores of Himanshu (who had a blocked nose) taken over, when a much louder holler erupted.

A clatter of hooves broke into the silence of the study. Was it coming from—was it possible—the History book? The pages of the History book flapped as a tiny stallion's hooves thundered across it, with an even tinier sword-bearing woman astride.

'Hates History?' the woman yelled, her royal nose

in the air. 'HATES HISTORY? What kind of helmetless clowns are these children of today? Would they even be here without history? I suggest we start a revolt against the students who revolt against History.'

'Er Ma'am, who are you?' asked someone from page 92 of the Civics book.

'Rani Lakshmibai of Jhansi!' She waved her sword furiously. 'I am no Ma'am sha'am. Call me Queen.'

A buzz cut her off almost instantly. The Rani turned mid-speech to see a hurricane of bees pouring out from within the Biology book. She swished her sword at them heroically. She'd taken on armies of soldiers, what were a few bees, ha!

'No, no, Queen,' cried the bees. 'We aren't here to harm you. We bees always protect the queen.'

At that, a more imperious, rather fat bee exploded on the scene. 'You idiots! I am your queen. I am the queen bee. Don't go running after other queens.'

'You are an insect,' Rani Lakshmibai pointed out. 'I am the only queen on this table.'

The Chemistry book suddenly flapped to life and a crusty old voice murmured, 'And I am the only table on this table. So will everyone stop arguing?'

'Table? Whose table? And why isn't it round?' called King Arthur of the Round Table, stepping out of a lesson in English literature that Akanksha had fallen asleep over. His armour clanged and he tugged at his cloak where it was stuck in the page. (Such inappropriate dressing for modern times!) 'And I, my dear queens, am a king!'

'I am the only table on this table. The Periodic Table,' insisted the crusty old voice, ignoring the great king. 'Within me are elements of a similar behaviour, quite unlike you folk. Let me introduce you to one of my most popular elements—aluminium. We call him good old Al.'

The Physics book almost jumped up, quivering in indignation. From its pages hopped a rather strange-looking man with droopy eyes and a huge forehead that resembled the hill in the Geography book's 'Land Formations' chapter. But most obvious of all was his hair. It sprang hither-thither like silver wires from his scalp—especially now that he looked most annoyed. 'Who called me? I have been sleeping for decades now. And I keep telling everyone not to call me Al. My name is Albert Einstein, nothing shorter please.'

'Who said they were calling you?' Another senior gentleman in a three-piece suit climbed out laboriously from the same Physics book. 'You always grab the limelight. Whereas it was I who invented the lamplight. You wouldn't even be able to see without my bulb,' said Thomas Alva Edison. 'Though I hate to be called Al too.'

While the three Als were in a heated discussion, the Art textbook opened and a soft light glowed from within its pages. The characters, who were strewn across the study table by then, stopped. A breathtakingly lovely lady in a white sari emerged from its pages. Her beautiful face glowed as her hand cupped the long brass lit diya she held. 'Was someone calling for light?' she asked shyly. 'I am a painting by Raja Ravi Verma, from the royal family of Travancore.'

'There you go,' declared Rani Lakshmibai to King Arthur. 'You're not the only king here. This lady comes from a Raja.'

'But I am a ruler!' protested King Arthur.

'So am I!' piped up an entirely new voice, bright and spunky. And the pencil-box snapped open while the footruler jumped up to attention. 'We rulers come in sizes of 6 or 12 inches.'

'Plenty of rulers and plenty of kings, you see!' smirked Rani Lakshmibai.

'Would you mind not swishing your sword about in my face?' bellowed King Arthur. 'You aren't the only one with a sword, you know? Mine even has a name. It's called Excalibur!'

'Ha! Whoever would name a sword?' scoffed the Rani. 'And whoever would make tables round? You come from a strange page indeed.'

The bees meanwhile were terribly confused. They had two queens and two kings and two rulers. Whom should they go buzz around? They swarmed from one corner of the study to the other. The Rani of Jhansi's horse kept dashing out of their way. He was a rather highly strung sort.

'If the speed of the bees is 59 km per hour and the speed of the horse is 43 km per hour, calculate the distance between them in a 100 square foot room,' yelled the Maths book gleefully, making the poor horse even more nervous.

'Huh!' scoffed the English book. 'You're a show-off! You just gas too much!'

'Gas is a mixture of hydrocarbons with the molecular formula C_2H_{12} to C_2H_{20},' the Chemistry book squeaked.

Thomas Alva Edison coughed a bit. 'Not to put anyone into the shade, but ahem, ahem...why go back to candle light? When I've already invented the bulb. See how bright it shines,' he climbed up the wall to switch on the overhead lamp in the study, when a ferocious roar punctured the air, and Mr Edison, or Al as he hated being called, almost fell right off. He dangled on a plug precariously, peeping down to see what the hullaballoo was all about.

To everyone's amazement, turning to panic, a flash of gold burst out of the English literature book. A royal Bengal tiger in all its majesty leapt out to the sound of a commanding voice which said, 'Tyger, tyger, burning bright. In the forests of the night; What immortal hand or eye, Could frame thy fearful symmetry? In what distant deeps or skies. Burnt the fire of thine eyes? On what wings dare he aspire? What the hand, dare seize the fire?—William Blake at your service, was someone talking about bright?'

'Her hand dares seize the fire,' pointed Rani Lakshmibai at the lady with the lamp. 'I am so tired of men taking all the credit.'

'And I am so tired of scientists taking all the limelight, or lamplight or bulb light or whatever!' shouted William Blake. 'Could any of you ever write poetry like this? You science types are all blind to such art!'

The Hindi grammar book could stay shut no longer. It had suffered these fools too long. It sprang open and from the *muhavre* page came a very deep (rather Mr Bachchan-like voice if you'd like to imagine it), '*Andha kya jaane basant ke bahar.*'

The computer which was left on, much to Mummy's annoyance every morning, suddenly beeped to life as well. Google Translate informed everyone, in its staccato tone, 'That translates as: What will the blind man know of spring's colours?'

'Are you calling us blind?' the Science books clamped together in a united stand and rushed forward towards the language books. 'Well, it's all very relative,' began Al Einstein, whose theory of relativity, as you know, caused quite a stir. But the books ignored the great man, and clashed together. The shock threw Thomas 'Al' Edison, who could hang on no longer by the tips of his fingernails, back down onto the study table right on top of the poor ruler, which snapped into two.

The bees who were extremely sensitive creatures, got very very agitated at this new turn of events and turn of switches and rise of the Science books and fall of the scientist and you know—all that—and they buzzed together hysterically in a thick black cloud, heading towards Mr Blake's Tyger. Tyger, who could take on any man or beast, was rather scared of insects as it happened (hadn't a fly once gotten into his ear?) and he leapt around, charging wildly at the pen stand on the table, which he knocked over, so that the pens flew like arrows in a 180 degree arc (or so the protractor claimed).

Rani Lakshmibai's horse had had it! All those bees were bad enough, now flying pens and charging tigers? No way! It was much better back in 1858. The horse galloped across the table, attempting to smash its way back into the pages of the History book where it belonged.

Al Einstein jumped away from its hooves just in time, his hair flying about even more. He landed plonk in the middle of the Pacific Ocean, which was the page on which the atlas was open. The atlas was a peaceful old book and not used to such violent attacks at all. The water from the Pacific Ocean splashed unhelpfully all over the Periodic Table, which was absolutely furious. 'H_2O should be kept in its own place. Do not mix everything up,' it howled.

Every character, historical or not, charged around fleeing water, bees, horse and Tyger.

In the middle of this all, the large grandfather clock in the hall struck five long chimes. Gong, gong, gong, gong, gong!

'*Panch!*' screamed the Hindi book.

King Arthur boxed the Hindi book with all his might. 'A rather heroic punch if I should say so myself,' he said proudly.

'But whyyyy?' cried the English book holding its friend, the Hindi book, with its now broken spine.

'Because the Hindi Book asked me to punch it.'

'*Panch,*' explained Google Translate, 'is Hindi for five. It is five o'clock. The family will soon rise.'

A hush descended upon the warring characters.

They eyed each other and the destruction across the study. Then, without a word, they dived back into their respective books.

Stumbling bleary-eyed into the study an hour later, Mummy shrieked, 'Have you been studying about historical battles, or fighting them in here?' she demanded of her children.

Himanshu and Akanksha stared in utter shock at their books which looked like they'd been drowned, stabbed, shredded and what-have-you.

'Does this mean we can't answer the exams?' asked Himanshu with a sudden gleam of hope.

'You most certainly have to,' Mummy was furious. 'I've heard of every excuse from you two. Now this. The ruler's in two pieces, the Hindi book's in three pieces, the Rani of Jhansi's sword has pierced the Greater Alps—and how on earth did you get a minuscule pug print across the symbol of Al?'

A small voice answered, 'I told you never to call me Al.'

Notes on Contributors

Andaleeb Wajid writes fiction for children, young adults and adults. Her novel *When She Went Away* was shortlisted for The Hindu Young World Goodbooks Award 2017. She has two sons, and both don't read her books, which is fortunate for her as she can write about their exploits and they will never even know.

Anshumani Ruddra lives in Bangalore with his wife and son and is deeply embedded in the Indian startup ecosystem. He predominantly writes speculative fiction and is the author of India's first multiplayer gamebook for young adults, *The Enemy of My Enemy*.

C.G. Salamander is a fiction writer and comic journalist who lives in Chennai with his dog Hazel. He's currently working on a book about dogs with magical powers.

Chatura Rao won The Hindu Young World Goodbooks Award 2018 for her picture book, *Gone Grandmother*.

She's authored several books and short stories for children and adults. She is the Director of the Chandigarh Children's Literature Festival. She loves to run, travel and juggle with words. Her motto in life is Stay Silly!

Deepa Agarwal is the award-winning author of over fifty books. Most of her stories arise from the world around her. A character in this story was inspired by one of her granddaughter's best friends.

Devika Rangachari is an award-winning children's writer whose book, *Queen of Ice* (Duckbill), was on the White Raven list of the best children's books from around the world in 2015. Her other books include *Tales of Love and Adventure* (Scholastic), *Swami Vivekananda—A Man with a Vision* (Puffin), *Harsha Vardhana* (Scholastic), *The Merry Mischief of Gopal Bhand* (Scholastic), *The Wit of Tenali Raman* (Scholastic) and *Growing Up* (Children's Book Trust; on the Honour List of the International Board on Books for Young People in 2002). Devika has just completed her post-doctoral research on gender in Indian history, and enjoys interacting with children and young adults, and convincing them that history is great fun.

Harshikaa Udasi is a Mumbai-based journalist who has worked with *The Hindu, The Week, Deccan Herald,* and *The Times of India.* She runs the Book Trotters Club, a reading club for children in Mumbai. Her first book for children, *Kittu's Very Mad Day*, published by Duckbill, features a protagonist who is disabled. She solemnly swears that her story 'Welcome Home, Sugar' was NOT written by an AI robot.

Jane De Suza has been called one of the funniest writers in India today, which is why she's moving to Singapore. Besides the popular SuperZero series, she's written other books, and for magazines and anthologies worldwide. She also writes a column for *The Hindu*. She loves animals even though they can't read her books.

Jerry Pinto is the author of the novels *Murder in Mahim* (2017) and *Em and the Big Hoom* (2012; winner of the Hindu Prize and the Crossword Book Award), and the non-fiction book *Helen: The Life and Times of an H-Bomb* (2006; winner of the National Award for the Best Book on Cinema). His children's books include *A Bear for Felicia*, *Monster Garden*, and *When Crows Are White*. In 2016, Jerry Pinto was awarded the Windham-Campbell Prize and the Sahitya Akademi Award.

Lavanya Karthik lives in Mumbai where she writes, draws, takes a lot of naps and talks to stray dogs. She is the author of several picture books and a series of illustrated middle-grade novels. Be warned, anything you say to her could be used in the comics she likes to draw between naps.

Menaka Raman is an occasional writer, runner and mother. When she's not drinking coffee she is trying to run away from her children's Maths homework.

Nandini Nayar is an award-winning children's writer with over forty books for children of all ages. She's written twenty-two picture books, over three hundred short stories, several novels, retellings and fictional biographies. For more information about her visit her website www.nandininayar.in

Payal Dhar has been making up stories all her life. Sometimes she has got into trouble for them, but some others have been published as novels and short stories, mostly for young people. She is the author of nine books, including *Slightly Burnt, Hit for a Six* and *A Helping Hand* (this one can be read for free at Storyweaver.org.in). She's also a freelance editor and writer, and writes on computers, technology, books, reading, games, travel and anything else that catches her interest. When nobody's looking, she either has her nose in a book, is surfing the Internet, or battling evil in a computer game. Visit Writeside.net to find out more about Payal's work and play.

Award-winning author **Roopa Pai** has written over twenty-five books for children, spanning the gamut from fiction to non-fiction and picture books to chapter books, on themes as varied as sci-fi fantasy, Maths, Science, Economics, Philosophy, History and life skills. When she isn't writing, this one-time computer engineer leads children on history and nature walks around her beloved hometown, as part of her day job with heritage walks and tours company, BangaloreWalks.

Shabnam Minwalla is a mother of three. In the little off-time that this brain-scrambling job permits, she writes books for children and articles for magazines and newspapers. Her books include the popular *Six Spellmakers of Dorabji Street* and *The Shy Supergirl*. Her new book *What Maya Saw* has been greeted with excellent reviews.

Shreekumar Varma's books for children include *The Royal Rebel*, *Devil's Garden* and *The Magic Store of Nu-Cham-Vu*. He has written numerous stories and articles for children. He is also a novelist, playwright, poet and reviewer.